"Done alr[...] when Erica put her tray down.

"For now. I talked to Mike. He's better-looking close-up than he is from far away, if you can believe it."

"Did he seem interested?" Kitty asked eagerly.

Erica took a long sip of her soda. "Mmm . . . I think so. Anyway, it doesn't matter if he's interested. I've decided I'm going to have him, so he doesn't have much of a choice."

"Hey, I give you credit for your ability to attract boys, but what do you mean, 'he doesn't have a choice?' How can you say that when he's already interested in Maddie?"

Erica's eyes grew dark. "You don't know me all that well, Kitty. I usually get what I want."

"Really?" Kitty asked.

"Yes, really," Erica answered, serious. "Besides, I have a plan."

Other books in the **ROOMMATES** series:

COMING SOON

Roommates

HIGHER EDUCATION
Alison Blair

Ivy Books
Published by Ballantine Books
Copyright © 1988 by Butterfield Press, Inc.

Produced by Butterfield Press, Inc.
133 Fifth Avenue
New York, New York 10003

IVY BOOKS • NEW YORK

Higher Education

Chapter 1

I'm back! Madison Lerner thought with excitement as the aging gray bus pulled into the Hawthorne Springs depot. Maddie peered out the grimy window, even though there wasn't much to see. But it didn't matter that Hawthorne Springs, Georgia, wasn't the most exciting place in the world. Maddie was just about to start her sophomore year at Hawthorne College, and she knew it was going to be great.

The bus had only been stopped for a few seconds, but already the passengers, mostly students, were filling the aisle. Maddie stood up and stretched, trying not to bump her head on the overhead luggage rack. She hadn't been sitting very long, only forty-five minutes since she had picked up the bus in Western Springs where she had been visiting her great-aunt. It didn't matter. Any amount of time spent cramped on a bus seat made Maddie feel like a sardine. She rubbed a place on her forearm that had fallen asleep.

When the girl she'd been sitting beside finally moved into the aisle, Maddie reached up and attempted to remove the huge, overstuffed plaid suitcase she had put on the overhead rack. It teetered dangerously on the edge, looking as if it was about to crash onto Maddie's head. Then suddenly, strong, muscular arms grabbed the suitcase and lowered it to the floor gracefully.

"There you go." A tall, very handsome boy smiled down at Maddie, but before she could even say thank you, he had vanished down the aisle and was almost off the bus. Maddie's eyes followed him closely.

Who is he? she wondered. She picked up her purse and headed down the aisle behind him.

Maddie could already feel the hot Georgia air. She hesitated on the bus steps, squinting into the sunshine. After the dark, cool bus, everything seemed much too bright.

"Maddie! Over here!"

Maddie looked around until she found Roni Davies waving wildly from her little red MG, parked behind a wire fence. After Maddie stepped off the bus, she ran as fast as she could toward Roni, with her suitcase banging against her leg.

Roni's auburn curls bounced wildly as she jumped out of the car and flung herself at

Maddie. "You made it!" she announced with a loud yell.

After a quick hug, Maddie wriggled her way out of Roni's enthusiastic embrace. "I didn't have a choice," she said dryly. "Classes start in two days, remember?"

Roni laughed, then held Maddie at arm's length and looked her over. "You cut your hair. I'm shocked."

Giving her new, close-cropped cut a nervous pat, Maddie said, "I just walked into a salon in Chicago one day and got it done. Spur-of-the-moment type thing. What do you think?"

"I think it's adorable," Roni cried. "You look like a little boy with that short hair and those big blue eyes."

Just then, the guy who had helped Maddie with her suitcase walked by. "See you around," he said with a generous smile.

Maddie was too surprised to say anything, but the minute he was out of earshot, Roni gasped, "Who was that gorgeous hunk?"

Maddie knew how Roni loved to dramatize things, so she didn't want to appear too interested. "Just someone who helped me with my bag."

Roni ruffled Maddie's hair. "Well, obviously, he thinks your hair looks pretty cute, too."

"Cute for a little boy," Maddie complained as she threw her suitcase into the back of the car.

"Cute for anyone," Roni replied, getting behind the wheel.

"So," Maddie said after Roni had roared out of the parking lot, "you finally got your car back." It had been a running joke last semester that the car Roni had brought to a local gas station for some small repairs had been lost in a Georgia swamp, and would never be seen again.

"'Finally' is right," Roni answered with disgust. "My father had to have it towed back to Atlanta and, believe me, he was not pleased."

"Well, it's great that you've got it now," Maddie said. "You'll be the coolest sophomore on campus." She ran her hands admiringly over the bright red leather interior. Roni's parents were wealthy Atlanta socialites who loved to lavish extravagant gifts on their daughter— although the presents always seemed to come with an emotional price tag.

Roni adjusted her tiger-striped sunglasses. "Yes, but I had to dress—as my father put it— like a *lady* the whole time I was home. Otherwise I was going to have to leave the car home for the year."

Roni was well known at Hawthorne for her outrageous style of dressing. Maddie often wondered where she came up with some of her outfits. Right now Roni was decked out in a short-sleeved turquoise shirt with French poodles prancing on it, black camp shorts, and turquoise sneakers. Maddie knew that Roni's parents wanted a demure debutante for a daughter; instead, they had one who looked as if she belonged on MTV.

"So, where are Stacy and Sam?" Maddie inquired. "When are they coming back?"

"We're meeting them at the dorm. Stacy drove all night from Boston, and she's picking Sam up at the train station. It seems like you two could have coordinated your schedules. Being from Illinois, I mean."

Maddie laughed. "Roni, you know I've been visiting my aunt for a couple of days. I took the local Atlanta bus here from Western Springs."

"Oh, right. I forgot." Roni shrugged. "How is your aunt Fitty, anyway?"

Maddie was very fond of her aunt, her great-aunt actually. She was grateful to Fitty for giving her a place to live when she had first come to Hawthorne and it had seemed as though Maddie would never find on-campus housing. "She's fine," Maddie answered, "but she is getting older and slowing down."

"I don't want to think about getting old"— Roni shuddered—"or slowing down." She put her foot on the gas to make her point. Within minutes, the girls were pulling up in front of their dorm, Rogers House.

Rogers House, where the girls had spent their freshman year, was the oldest dorm on the Hawthorne Campus. In many ways, its age was part of its charm. Tall spires and french windows gave the stone building a castle-like appearance. But inside, the suites, each with a living room, two bedrooms, and two small baths, were tired looking and furnished with faded and mismatched furniture—most of it in a horrible plaid. And as the girls found out at the end of the spring semester, the building had not been very safe, either. Worn-out wiring had caused a fire in their suite, and it was mostly luck that Maddie had smelled the smoke in time to get her roommates out of the burning area.

But today, Rogers House was no longer just a silent stone fortress. Scaffolding surrounded the sides of the building, and workmen were laughing and joking as they used jackhammers and chisels on the exterior.

"Oh, wow," Roni breathed. "Do you suppose they're tearing it down?"

"Don't be silly. They're cleaning it up."

"Let's see if they're doing anything to the inside," Roni said eagerly. "That's where they need to use those chisels, hacking off fifty years of dirt."

Leaving their suitcases in the car, Roni and Maddie hurried up the cobblestone walk to the front door. But before they could go inside, Pam, the dorm's head resident this year, came barreling out and almost bumped into them.

"Oh, Roni and Maddie, welcome back," she greeted them with a distracted smile.

"What's going on, Pam?" Roni asked, her eyes wandering to one of the younger workmen perched on the scaffold. "We have company. How long are they going to be looking in our windows?"

"Roni, you haven't changed," Pam said, shaking her head. "Actually, this was all supposed to be finished yesterday, but the foreman promised the housing office they'd be out of here in a day or two."

"I guess they're fixing the wiring and stuff, right?" Maddie said.

Pam ran a hand through her curly hair. "That's not the half of it. After the fire, one of our wealthy alums, a Mrs. Wentworth, decided Rogers House was a disgrace. She wanted to 'restore it to its former glory,' as she put it."

"Really," Maddie said, impressed.

"So she donated a very sizable sum of money for doing just that. They've been redoing the interior all summer, and now the crews are finishing up on the outside."

"You're kidding! You mean they've actually redecorated our suites?" Roni asked, more than a hint of scepticism in her voice.

Pam nodded. "It's a regular *Architectural Digest* layout in there."

"Well, let's take a look at it," Roni said eagerly.

"Not just yet." Pam put up a restraining hand. "You can put your luggage over there if you want," she said, pointing to a wire enclosure piled high with trunks and bags, "but we're not quite ready for people to move in yet. There are going to be some changes in the dorm, and we have to talk to all the residents together."

Maddie didn't like the serious expression on Pam's face. "What kind of changes?"

"Not now," Pam said. "I have to go to the

housing office and pick up some invoices. Just get back here in an hour."

Before the girls could question her any further, Pam gave them a wave and hurried away.

"I can't believe it," Roni said, staring up at the building. "Here we thought we were going to be stuck in grungy old Rogers House, and it turns out we'll be living in the lap of luxury."

"Do you think it could really be as nice as Pam says?"

"We'll find out, I guess." Roni glanced at her watch. "Well, what now? Got any ideas on how to kill an hour?"

"Maybe we should just hang around here," Maddie offered tentatively. "Stacy and Sam won't know where to find us if we take off."

"Hey, no problem. There they are now." Roni, shading her eyes, pointed down the road where a silver Mercedes was leaving a trail of dust in its wake.

The car screeched to a halt, and Stacy Swanson and Samantha Hill jumped out. They ran over to Roni and Maddie, and the air was instantly full of shrieks, hugs, and kisses.

"Stacy, you look wonderful," Maddie said, taking in her lean and elegant roommate. "You got a great tan on the Vineyard!"

Stacy touched her blond hair. "Maddie, your hair is almost as short as mine!"

"Yeah, but you look like a fashion model. Roni tells me I look like a little boy."

"An adorable little boy," Roni put in.

"What about me?" Sam asked. "Don't I look wonderful?"

Maddie smiled at Sam. "You look exactly the same, and that's wonderful."

Sam frowned. "I should have cut my hair."

"Oh no," Stacy said. "Long, straight hair is just right for you."

"I'm too preppy," Sam fretted. "I should have dyed my hair, not just cut it. Like the time Stacy dyed her hair pink."

Maddie giggled.

"We're back on campus five minutes and we have to start talking about that?" Stacy groaned. "Come on, let's find our suite and stow our bags. I want to get my suitcase unpacked before some trunks of mine arrive."

"No can do, Stace," Roni informed her.

"Why not?"

"They're not quite finished the make-over of Roger's House."

Sam glanced over at the building. "I saw the workmen. What's this all about?"

"It's a surprise," Roni replied, "but I'm starving. Why don't we drive over to PizzaRoo, and I'll tell you about it on the way?"

"Sounds good to me," Sam said. "I missed breakfast on the train."

After dumping their bags in the designated area, all four girls climbed into Stacy's car and drove over to the local pizza parlor and all-round campus hangout—the PizzaRoo.

The owners had attempted to achieve an

Italian decor. Faded red-and-white-checked cloths were on the tables, and posters of Venice, Florence, and Rome lined the walls. But the main attraction at PizzaRoo was the hot, cheesy deep-dish pizza lavished with sausage and tomatoes. The pizza provided a welcome alternative to the food served in the Commons dining room where most of the students ate. At the moment, the PizzaRoo was crawling with students, but Maddie spotted an empty table in the back and Roni, Stacy, and Sam followed behind her, squeezing themselves into the corner where the rickety table stood.

"Don't tell me you've forgotten what's on the menu," Roni laughed as Sam scanned the stained piece of cardboard she had plucked from behind the napkin dispenser. "We've only been gone a couple of weeks."

"Yes, but eating my mother's wonderful cooking has blotted out all memory of other food," Sam declared.

"That sounds nice," Stacy said a little wistfully.

"How is Sydney?" Maddie asked. She knew that Stacy's mother was often a thorn in Stacy's side. Sydney had been especially troublesome since the break-up of her fourth marriage.

Stacy shrugged. "All right, I guess. She's handling the divorce better than either one of us thought she would. As a matter of fact, after making such a big deal about my coming to the

Vineyard to comfort her, Sydney went off to a spa for four days and left me alone."

"She didn't!" Maddie exclaimed.

"Typical Sydney," Stacy informed her. "I went over to my dad's house and stayed with him."

"Have you seen Pete yet?" Roni asked.

Stacy's blue eyes softened at the mention of her ex-boyfriend's name. "No, but I talked to him last night, and we might get together to talk tonight or tomorrow. I hope we can still be friends, but I don't know." Stacy sighed.

After giving their order to the waitress, Roni turned the conversation back to boys. "Well, since I broke up with Zack, I'm as free as a bird."

"What about me?" Maddie cut in. "I got a letter from Stu last week saying he's going to school at home this year, and that he hopes we'll stay in touch."

"You're kidding!" Stacy said. "That's terrible."

Maddie snapped her fingers. "Gone with the wind," she said brightly; but the truth was, the prospect of starting her sophomore year without Stu was a downer.

"Well, Aaron and I are definitely finished, so that leaves four out of four roommates without men," Sam commented glumly.

"Come on, we'll all be dating new guys in no time," Stacy said encouragingly.

"Easy for you to say," Maddie pointed out.

"There was that guy eyeing you at the bus station," Roni reminded her. "Or have you forgotten him already?"

"Really?" Sam said with interest.

"He wasn't eyeing me," Maddie protested. Even though his handsome face had been in the back of her mind since he first smiled at her, Maddie wanted to downplay the whole thing. But Roni was not about to let it go.

"You should have seen him. Tall, with a terrific build, dark hair . . ."

"I suppose you even noticed his eyes," Maddie said, laughing in spite of herself.

"Gray. Kind of blue-gray," Roni said promptly.

Stacy and Sam were about to ask for more details when the waitress brought their drinks, interrupting the conversation.

"Well," Maddie said, trying to change the subject, "if we're not going to be dating, at least we'll enjoy our solitude in gorgeous new suites, thanks to Mrs. Wentworth."

"When are we supposed to view our glamorous new digs?" Sam asked.

Roni swallowed a sip of her Coke. "Pam said to be back in an hour," she answered casually.

A look of concern passed over Sam's face. "But we've almost been gone an hour already, and we haven't even eaten yet."

"You worry too much," Roni said. "So we get back a little late. What difference could it make?"

But when the girls straggled back to the dorm, Pam was waiting for them, a sour look on her face. "I thought I told you to be back for the meeting."

"We're sorry," Maddie apologized.

"We were so hungry. . . ." Sam's words faded away as she and the other girls followed Pam into the reception area.

"I don't believe this," Stacy said, craning her neck.

Sam, too, was looking around. "It's beautiful," she said, nodding in agreement, her blue eyes wide.

"It sure is." Maddie could hardly believe this was Rogers House. The flowered chintz furniture had been replaced by sleek tangerine-and-teal print sofas and chairs. The walls, which used to be an indescribable mud color, were now an airy gray, and the wooden reception counter had been restored and polished back to its former glory.

"Talk about before and after," Stacy said. "I hope someone took pictures. Otherwise no one would believe it."

Roni's green eyes sparkled with excitement. "Take us upstairs, Pam, and show us our suite. If it looks anything like this, it should be dyna-mite."

Maddie nodded her head in agreement. Her room back home was great, but with all the ruffles and flowers it made her feel like she was still a little girl. It seemed as though whoever had designed the interior of Roger's House understood that college girls needed a little more sophistication. "Are we going to be on the second floor again?" she asked.

Pam looked serious, and Maddie, for the life of her, couldn't figure out why. *What could be so terrible when they'd be living in a place like this?*

Chewing on her lip nervously, Pam said, "Look, I know you all have been through an awful lot together, but the fact is we can't put the four of you in one suite. I'm afraid we're going to have to split you up."

Chapter 2

Maddie couldn't believe her ears. Not room together? Living with Roni, Stacy and Sam was one of the best things about being at college. She was just about to protest when Roni beat her to it.

"What do you mean, Pam? We signed up to room together, and housing always okays those requests," Roni said angrily.

"Is it because of the fire?" Sam asked. "It wasn't our fault, you know. The fire chief said it was caused by old wiring."

"It has nothing to do with the fire."

"Look," Stacy began, "I know we were noisy sometimes, but . . ."

"This has nothing to do with you personally at

15

all," Pam said patiently. "Let's sit down and I'll explain." The girls followed her over to one of the handsome sofas, away from the main traffic area.

Roni crossed her legs and folded her arms in front of her. "All right, if it's not about us personally, what's the deal?"

"If you had been here for the meeting," Pam said, a stern edge coming into her voice, "You'd know what the deal is. When Mrs. Wentworth donated the money for the renovation, she also stipulated that the dorm institute some sort of residential Big Sister program."

"Big Sisters?" Maddie asked, confused.

"Yes. Apparently when she was at Hawthorne in 1947, there was an arrangement where the sophomores looked out for the freshmen."

Maddie looked in Roni's direction and had to stifle a giggle. Roni was wrinkling her nose as though watching out for freshman were only one step above hauling garbage.

"So," Pam continued, "since we already have a sizable number of sophomores and freshmen signed up for this dorm, the housing office decided to fulfill Mrs. Wentworth's requirement by putting two freshmen and two sophomores in each suite."

"Then at least two of us can be together?" Sam asked, looking around at her friends.

"Yes. You four can divide up any way you like."

"Are you sure there can't be an exception?"

Roni asked. "Isn't there one suite you can put us all in?"

"It can be the crummiest one you've got," Stacy chimed in.

"Sorry, there aren't any crummy suites. And there aren't any exceptions."

The girls looked at each other: Stuck was stuck.

"Well," Stacy said tentatively, "how do you want to divide up?"

Roni shook her head. "I don't know."

Sam turned pleading eyes on Pam. "Maybe there's a suite in some other dorm. I wouldn't mind giving up all this luxury if we could stay together."

"Neither would I," Maddie agreed, and Stacy and Roni were nodding vigorously as well.

"Sorry," Pam said sympathetically, "but there are no other dorms open. Housing has a waiting list. Listen, it won't be too bad. The two freshman suites I have open are just down the hall from each other."

"Well, that's something," Roni muttered.

Maddie nervously tugged at her hair. "Pam, why don't *you* just divide us up? It's too hard for us to make a big decision like that."

"Uh-uh. I'm not getting in the middle of this. What if you guys have a big blow-up in the middle of the semester? You'll blame it on me."

"Us fight?" Roni asked, wide-eyed.

Even Maddie had to laugh at that. She remembered too well the arguments last semester that had ended with none of them speaking to one another. Fortunately, it had all worked out, but obviously Pam remembered it well, too.

"Look, Pam, write down all our names on pieces of paper and one of us will pick them from your hand," Sam suggested. "That way it'll all be left to chance."

Pam looked around the circle. "Is that okay with everyone?"

Maddie nodded and Roni, in a resigned voice muttered, "I guess."

"It's the only way," Stacy added. "I don't know how we'd decide otherwise."

As Pam took out a pencil from her shirt pocket and began tearing into strips a piece of paper she found on the table, Maddie's eyes wandered to each of her friends. She tried to decide whom she'd room with if she had to choose. There was no doubt she felt the strongest connection to Sam. Level-headed and down to earth, Sam was like Maddie in many ways. They were the kind of friends who didn't always have to be talking if they were alone together: Each seemed to know what the other was thinking. Of course, she and Stacy were sorority sisters in Alpha Pi Alpha, and that forged a special bond between them. When Maddie had first met Stacy she had been slightly in awe of her. Stacy looked more as though she belonged on the cover of *Seventeen* or *Glamour* than hanging around Hawthorne Springs going to a small, liberal arts college. But after living with Stacy, Maddie now knew that she was a lot less secure than she appeared. Divorced parents and eating disorders were Stacy's devils, although she was much more in control of herself than she had been last year.

Then there was Roni. A smile crept to Maddie's lips. She and Roni were at the opposite ends of the world, in appearance and temperment, but they had shared a room last semester and after a few major stumbles, they had finally come to terms with their differences. Living in the same suite this summer had been a breeze, and Maddie was sure that sharing a room with Roni would work out fine, too.

"All right," Pam said briskly, putting down her pencil. "I've got all your names here." She opened her hand and showed them four neatly folded scraps of paper. "Sam, pick one."

Sam reached out a tentative hand and chose a name. "Roni," she read.

"That's it then," Pam said, getting up. "Sam and Roni, which leaves Maddie and Stacy."

Maddie smiled over at Stacy. "Looks like you're stuck with me."

Stacy made a face. "It's not *you* I'm worried about. Pam, do you know which freshmen we'll be living with?"

"Let me check." Pam walked over to the reception desk and looked down at the clipboard. "I'm going to put you and Maddie in with Jean Jones and Erica Martin."

Jean and Erica. Maddie tried to form a mental

picture, but nothing came to mind. "What are they like?" she asked nervously.

"Let's go meet them and find out," Stacy replied.

"How about us?" Roni demanded.

"You're with Liz Armstrong and Angela Perelli. I know for a fact they've gone out, so I'll just give you the keys for suite 3D and you can wait for them."

"That reminds me," Sam piped up, "just what does this Big Sister program entail?"

"We don't have to drag them around campus with us, do we?" Roni asked.

"We talked about that at the orientation," Pam said pointedly. "No one expects you to be best friends with these girls, but we would like you to make their lives a little easier here. Show them around, introduce them to people. Tell them how to get involved in activities."

"I guess that sounds all right," Roni agreed grudgingly. "But I'm not introducing them to any cute guys. If I ever see one of those around here, he's all mine!"

Pam laughed as she led Maddie and Stacy upstairs. "That Roni, she never changes."

Maddie felt her stomach flutter as she climbed the stairs to the third floor. She tried to calm down by reminding herself that she was the sophomore; they were only freshmen. If anyone should be nervous, it ought to be Jean and Erica. Actually, if she had one wish, it would be that they would all be friends. Roommates were such an important part of college life. It would be terrible to be stuck with someone you didn't really like.

Pam knocked at the door. No one answered, but it swung open slowly. Maddie's eyes opened wide and all thoughts of her roommates flew out of her head. Although this suite had exactly the same layout as the one the girls had shared last year, if Maddie hadn't known she was standing in Rogers House, she never would have recognized it.

Gone was the broken-down furniture and peeling paint. Instead, scaled-down versions of the teal-and-tangerine furniture in the reception area decorated the living room. Built into the kitchen area was a gleaming white counter that housed a coffee maker, a beautiful sink with all new fixtures, and a compact refrigerator was tucked underneath. The French windows which led out to a small balcony were covered with pale teal drapes, but the girls could see a small white wrought-iron table and four chairs out-side.

"I think I've died and gone to heaven," Stacy said, blinking.

"What about the mice?" Maddie asked. Last year the mouse population in Roger's House seemed as though it had outnumbered the residents five to one.

"Gone." Pam snapped her fingers. "The exter-minators have been here for weeks. Mrs. Wentworth said she was hardly going to provide such luxurious surroundings for a horde of rodents."

"A woman after my own heart," Maddie said fervently.

"Excuse me? Can I help you?"

Maddie turned, and there, standing in the door of the bedroom was one of the cutest girls she had ever seen. Her chocolate-colored eyes were large and wide, and her dark, dark hair fell in perfect waves past her shoulders. The girl's white shorts and halter top showed off her curvy figure perfectly. *No one will have to introduce this freshman to boys,* Maddie thought to herself. *They'll be beating down the doors.*

"Hi, Erica, I'm Pam, the head resident."

"Oh, of course," Erica answered. "I knew you looked familiar, but I've just been meeting so many people today."

"Well, now I have two more for you. Important ones. Erica Martin, these are your other two rommates, Maddie Lerner and Stacy Swanson.

"Hello." Erica's rosebud mouth curved into a smile. "It's so nice to meet you."

"Where's Jean?" Pam asked.

"I don't know." Erica shrugged.

Maddie cocked her head toward the second bedroom. "It sounds like she's in the shower."

"Well, you'll get acquainted soon enough," Pam said. "I'm going to leave now, but don't forget there's going to be a little get-together tonight in the rec room at about eight." At the door, she waved and left the suite, shutting the door firmly behind her.

Maddie again reminded herself that as a sophomore she should feel calm and in control, but Erica's poise was throwing her a bit. Right now Erica was gesturing to the couch as though Maddie and Stacy were guests in her home. "Why don't we all sit down," she said graciously.

"Doesn't the room look great?" Maddie ventured.

Erica frowned slightly. "Do you really like those drapes? I think the material's a little shiny."

Stacy laughed out loud and then covered her mouth with her hand. "Sorry, but you should have seen this dorm last year. The drapes had so many holes in them we couldn't tell if the material was shiny or not."

"And the furniture was practically popping its springs," Maddie added.

"Really? They said the dorm was being renovated, but I had no idea." Erica glanced around the room as though seeing it in a completely different light.

Maddie wanted to impress Erica even further with her good fortune. "Let's just hope that Pam was right and all the mice are gone."

"Mice?" Erica shuddered. "You've got to be joking."

"Nope. Every suite came equipped with a family of five."

"But why did you stand for it?" Erica asked.

There was something about the directness of the question that stopped Maddie in her tracks and she could see the question was giving Stacy pause, too.

"Well," Stacy began slowly, "all the dorms were filled and we couldn't move. I guess it just seemed like a part of college life."

"I see," Erica answered, but Maddie could tell she didn't understand at all. Come to think of it, why *had* they put up with things like mice and peeling paint without even once complaining to the housing office? Erica would have complained. Even though they'd just met, Maddie was sure of that.

"So, where are you from, Erica?" Stacy asked.

"New York City. Well, in the winter anyway. During the summer we go to our house in the Hamptons."

"Where did you go to high school?"

"Cambridge Prep."

"Cambridge? I have a cousin who goes there," Stacy said. "Stephanie Sinclair."

Erica clapped her delicate hands together. "Stephanie? I've gone to dance class with her since we were in kindergarten, practically. Are you from New York, too?" she asked Stacy.

"No. I'm from Boston. And Maddie's from Chicago."

"Evanston," Maddie corrected. "My parents teach at Northwestern, but it's right outside the city."

"This is terrific." Erica's eyes sparkled. "We're all from big cities. I was afraid when I decided on Hawthorne that I'd be surrounded by people from Georgia." She didn't exactly grimace, but Maddie could tell the thought displeased her somewhat.

"I felt the same way last year, but it's nothing to worry about," Stacy assured her. "Hawthorne has a fine reputation, and there are kids here from all over. I even ended up with a Southern boyfriend."

"Really?" Erica commented with surprise. "Of course, I know you come to college to meet different kinds of people. But still, it's so great to have roommates who come from the same kind of background."

Maddie wasn't so sure this was true. Stacy was social register all the way, and apparently the same was true of Erica. But she was the daughter of two professors. From a city, yes, but hardly in the same class.

"That is, except for Jean," Erica said as she gestured toward the bedroom where the pounding of the shower water had stopped.

"What's Jean like?" Maddie asked curiously.

"Well, she's big."

Maddie looked to see if Erica was joking, but her expression was perfectly serious. "You mean she's overweight?"

"Not exactly."

Before Maddie could ask Erica to explain, the door to the bedroom opened and Maddie was faced with one of the tallest girls she had ever seen. Jean was at least six feet tall and solid. Even under her terry-cloth robe, it was obvious that Jean had a muscular build. She brushed her short dark hair out of her eyes, loped over to the couch, and stuck out her hand. "I'm Jean Jones," she said to Maddie.

Maddie couldn't remember the last time she had shaken hands with someone her own age, but, faced with Jean's outstretched hand, she gave it a perfunctory shake. "Maddie Lerner," she introduced herself.

"And I'm Stacy Swanson."

Jean sat down on one of the chairs, and a few drips of water from her wet hair sprinkled onto its arms. "Erica and I were wondering when you were going to arrive."

"We were . . . detained," Maddie answered.

"Where are you from?" Stacy asked conversationally.

"Idaho."

"That's a long way away," Maddie said politely. "How did you ever find your way here?"

"I'm on a basketball scholarship."

"Do we have a girl's basketball team?" Stacy asked, confused. "I don't think I've ever heard anything about one."

"Oh, it's been here, but it's not very good. I intend to change all that," Jean said confidently.

"That's nice," Maddie said. She couldn't think of any other comment to make.

"By the way," Stacy interjected smoothly. "I

noticed that each of you have taken one of the bedrooms, but Maddie and I were planning to room together. I'm sure you wouldn't mind doubling up so Maddie and I can share."

Maddie looked at Stacy with admiration. The same thought had occurred to her ever since they had walked into the room, but she never would have had the guts to say it.

Jean shrugged. "Hey, no problem."

Erica looked a little trapped, but she rearranged her features into a smile. "No, of course we don't mind. If that's what you want."

"We really appreciate it," Maddie said sincerely.

"Yes, we do." Stacy smiled. "I think this is going to work out just fine."

Roni had only just gotten a taste of the situation, but already she was convinced it would never work. The suite itself was great. Roni and Sam had been admiring it as they walked through the living room, when Roni had suddenly sniffed something strange. "What's that funny smell?"

Sam made a face. "It's terrible," she agreed.

"It's incense," a voice behind them announced. Both girls whirled around, and there at the open front door stood a girl who looked as though she had just stepped out of a movie set in the sixties. Red-gold curls swirled in spirals down to the small of her back. Her tie-dyed shirt was topped by a cranberry velvet vest, and she wore a long flowered skirt that swept her ankles and touched the top of her worn leather sandals. Thin, with huge blue eyes, the girl seemed more like a child playing dress-up than a college freshman. "Do you live here?" she asked politely.

"Uh, yes," Sam answered, embarrassed. "I'm Samantha Hill and this is Roni Davies. Call me Sam."

"Nice to meet you. I'm Angela—Angie—Perelli. Would you like a cup of herb tea?"

"I don't think so," Roni said. Sam shook her head as well.

Angie floated over to a hot plate. "I always have a cup of chamomile tea before I meditate."

Roni wasn't sure she had heard correctly. "What do you meditate about?"

"When you meditate you clear your mind," Angie explained as she added hot water to a purple mug covered with stars and moons. "You don't think about anything."

"Then why bother to do it?" Roni asked. She had little patience with what she thought was metaphysical nonsense.

"It helps you get in touch with your inner self."

"I have enough trouble fixing my hair on my outer self," Roni muttered.

"Well, if you'll excuse me," Angie said, "I like to stick to a schedule. I think I'll do my meditation on the balcony since it's so nice out."

"Nice?" Sam questioned. "It's pretty hot."

"I'm from Berkeley, and it gets cool there. I like this. It's different." She gave them a soft smile and turned toward the balcony. "Oh, by the way, Liz and I took the room on the left. I hope that's all right."

"Fine," Roni replied, relieved that at least she wouldn't have to share a room with this hippie.

"Where is Liz?" Sam inquired.

"I think she just went for a walk around campus. I'm sure she'll be back soon."

Once Angie was outside and settled in the lotus postion, Roni repeated out loud the words that had been going around and around in her head. "This isn't going to work."

Sam seemed concerned, but not devastated. "All right, maybe she's a little different, but she seems nice enough."

"Incense? Meditation? And did you see her outfit? Boy, people say *I* dress outrageously."

"The incense has got to go," Sam agreed, walking over to the brass holder where a jasmine scent wafted into the air. She carefully lifted the cone of incense and stuck it under the water tap. "But it's fun to meet different kinds of people, don't you think?" Sam coaxed.

"How in the world do you suppose she found her way here?" Roni asked, deliberately ignoring Sam's question.

"I haven't got the faintest idea."

"Maybe she's been in a time warp for twenty years."

Sam moved back to the couch and sat across from Roni. "You know, I feel a little sorry for Angie. It's not going to be easy for her here on campus."

Their conversation was interrupted by a shy knock on the outside of their still open door. "Come in," Sam called.

An attractive black girl stepped inside. "I'm Liz Armstrong and I live here, but I heard you talking so I didn't want to barge in. . . ."

Sam gave Liz a friendly smile. "Hi, I'm Samantha Hill. Everybody calls me Sam. We're your other roommates."

After her experience with Angie, Roni was wary. "I'm Roni Davies," she said curtly.

"Yes, I know," Liz said taking a seat on the arm of one of the chairs.

"You do?" Roni reacted with surprise.

"I went to Bloomfield Country Day, too."

"Sorry, I don't remember you," Roni said with embarrassment.

"No reason you should. I was two years behind you, but I took some accelerated classes and went to summer school for three years, so I made it here a year early."

"Why did you decide on Hawthorne?" Sam asked.

Liz gave a small shrug. "This is the school that gave me the best scholarship. I was a scholarship student at Bloomfield, too."

"Oh, you *were* . . ." Roni bit her lip.

"That's right, I was with the group of ten

minority students that got scholarships every year."

For a moment there was an awkward silence. Then Sam asked, "Have you met Angela yet?"

Liz smiled. "Yes. She's quite an anthropological discovery."

"She's a throwback to another era, all right," Roni said.

"Well, she'll add some spice to the campus," Sam commented.

Roni mentally shook her head. Sam, the eternal optimist. She couldn't wait for Maddie and Stacy to meet Angie. She wondered what the luck of the draw had thrown their way.

What with unpacking and buying books, it wasn't until the Rogers House get-together later that evening that Roni, Stacy, Sam, and Maddie really had a chance to compare notes.

"You know we should be mingling," Sam said as she placed her soft drink on the new white table in the back of the rec room.

Roni took a bowl of pretzels off an adjoining table and set it down on the middle of their own. "We should," she agreed, settling in.

"I've already met a lot of people today," Maddie said. "Mostly freshmen."

Stacy pulled up a chair. "So, let's get to the most important people we've met today: our roommates."

Sam looked toward the center of the room

where Liz was standing by herself. "Liz is really nice."

Stacy glanced over at her. "She's pretty, too. I wish I had those dimples."

"Swanson, you're not the dimple type." Roni giggled. "Oh, maybe one discreet little dimple, but that's it. Now, Erica Martin must have a dimple or two," she added.

"She sure is cute." Maddie's eyes wandered over to the center of the room where Erica was surrounded by a group of girls. "She's not going to need us to show her around." Maddie had spent the afternoon watching Erica efficiently hang up her seemingly endless supply of clothes. Then Erica had placed silver-framed pictures of her family around her room. It was hard not to feel a little envious of someone who had her act so together.

"Jean, on the other hand, is going to have some problems," Sam predicted.

"She's actually very graceful for such a big girl," Roni said as she watched her moving toward a table piled with cakes, cookies, and soft drinks.

"She's a basketball player, don't forget," Maddie pointed out.

"I couldn't forget." Stacy sighed. "She's been telling me about plays all afternoon."

Maddie looked around the room. "What I want to know is, where is this Angela of yours? There's certainly no one here who fits her description."

Roni bit into a pretzel gloomily. "Oh, you'd know her if you saw her. She'd be the one chanting her mantra."

It was obvious to Maddie that Roni was really bothered by Angie, which was strange. If anyone was "live and let live," it was Roni. She spoke up gingerly. "Roni, so what if Angie is some sort of a flower child? You're not exactly Miss Preppy."

"I know, but between Angie and Liz . . . "

"Liz?" Sam asked with surprise. "What's wrong with Liz? I thought she was very nice."

"She is. Oh, never mind."

All the girls were silent a moment. Then Stacy said tentatively, "You said Liz went to your school. Did you know her then?"

Roni shook her head. "I really don't remember her at all. But I'm sure she's incredibly bright. All the scholarship students were."

"And she's got a Hawthorne academic scholarship," Maddie pointed out. "It's hard to get one of those."

"Look, she's a nice, smart kid and Angie seems a little dippy, but I'm sure she's a nice, smart kid, too," Roni answered crossly. "I'm getting some cake." She got up and stalked away.

"Whew," Sam said. "What's with her?"

"You tell us," Stacy said. "You were with her most of the day. Is she really that upset about Liz and Angie?"

"You know Roni, she does get moody sometimes," Maddie said. But in her heart Maddie felt this was more than one of Roni's bad moods. She seemed really unhappy about something.

"I talked to Roni while she was in Atlanta," Stacy said thoughtfully. "Her parents were giving her a really rough time those few weeks."

"What else is new?" Sam asked. "She goes home and the fireworks start."

"She told me living with the three of us last year gave her a real sense of security." Stacy added.

Maddie looked over at Roni, who was locked in conversation with Janet Fishbein. She still wore a sour expression. "And now she's got to adjust to two new roommates."

"Life's about adjustment," Sam said philosophically.

"True enough," Stacy agreed. "And we're adaptable."

Maddie nodded, but she could certainly sympathize with Roni. She also wished things could be just the way they used to be. Different roommates, no Stu. . . . Why did she have to adapt to so many things at once?

Chapter 3

No matter how many times Maddie took this walk, she was always impressed with the beauty of the Hawthorne campus. The most distinctive feature of the extensive landscaping was the large, man-made lake set off between the dorms and the quad. On this sultry day, ducks were swimming lazily through the water while students strolled around the lake holding hands.

Maddie sighed as she sat down on one of the stone benches near the water's edge. There was no denying it, she really missed Stu. Not that either one of them had thought of their relationship as permanent, but they did have lots of fun together. Stu was a great person to hang out with, romantic in his own soft, shy way and a very good friend, always ready to listen to

Maddie's problems. Looking around her, she felt
as though everyone in the school was already
matched up except her. Whoever said one was
the loneliest number hit the nail on the head.

As an only child Maddie had always felt like
the odd man out. Oh, her parents were great, if
somewhat overprotective, but that wasn't the
same as having brothers and sisters to grow up
with. That was one reason that her roommates
meant so much to her: They were just like the
sisters she had never had.

At first, Maddie had hoped she would develop
the same kind of closeness with Jean and Erica,
but that didn't seem very likely now. She certainly couldn't see herself becoming very close to
Jean. In the few days they had roomed together,
it had become obvious they had nothing in
common. She doubted anyone would find common ground with Jean—except maybe one of
the Boston Celtics or L.A. Lakers. Jean ate and
slept sports: It was a miracle she had time for
classes.

Erica was a different story. She seemed so
sweet and eager to please, but there was also a
sureness and sophistication about her that
Maddie envied. There was probably a lot she
could learn from Erica Martin.

"A penny for your thoughts."

Maddie looked up and saw Roni peering down
at her.

"Am I interrupting some wonderful day-
dream?" Roni asked.

"Not really. I should be thinking about how to reschedule my chem class so I don't have to run all the way across campus to make Chaucer, which starts ten minutes later."

"Sounds fascinating." Roni sat down beside her.

"How are you doing? You seemed kind of upset at that dorm thing, and I've barely seen you since then."

"I know. Not quite like when we were bumping into each other in the bathroom every morning."

"The good old days—don't remind me. But you didn't answer my question. How are you?"

"Fine," Roni said, but her tone belied her words.

"What's happening in Suite 3D?"

"Not much. Liz and Angela are model students. Angela studies and meditates. She informed me she's working on her mind and spirit. And Liz jogs and studies, so I guess she's working on her body and mind."

"Well, that all sounds commendable," Maddie said, confused by Roni's irritable tone.

"Yeah, it's great. And naturally, I haven't seen hide nor hair of anything remotely resembling a good-looking male."

"I can certainly sympathize on that score," Maddie said, twisting a corner of her white T-shirt. "I was just sitting here thinking about how much I miss Stu."

Roni picked up a few pebbles from the ground

and began tossing them back and forth in her hands. "There's some sort of party tonight. Do you want to go?"

"I guess," Maddie replied unenthusiastically.

Roni smiled slightly. "Boy, we're kind of pathetic."

"We sure are. Instead of feeling sorry for ourselves, we should be doing something. Then we'd feel better."

"Like?"

Maddie shrugged. "I don't know. Getting part-time jobs, reading books, solving world hunger."

"That would be a start."

"No, seriously. Here we are, not even a week into our sophomore year at college and we're totally bummed out. We're letting circumstances rule our lives. Okay, so we can't be roommates and we don't have boyfriends at this exact moment, but we can't let that ruin everything for us." Maddie stood up resolutely.

"Where are you going?" Roni asked, confused.

"No one is just going to fix my life up for me, so I'm going to do it myself. I really had fun working with the theater group last year, and I'm going to see if I can get involved with them again. Do you want to come along?"

Roni shook her head. "No, theater group isn't my thing."

"Well, I'm going to take off, okay?" Maddie was filled with purpose. "The sooner I get out of this pathetic state, the better."

With a little wave, Maddie left and began

walking toward the Fine Arts Complex. Last year she had had a big problem with juggling all her activities, and she was leery about taking on too much this semester. But when it came to the theater group, Maddie just couldn't resist.

The truth of the matter was, Maddie was a frustrated actress. As a small child she had taken singing and dancing lessons and had participated in all the school plays. Maddie never felt more alive than when she was on the stage performing, but when she had gotten to high school something had happened. Self-conscious about her looks and her changing body, Maddie had suddenly decided she didn't like being the center of attention on stage.

But last semester at Hawthorne Maddie had begun to get involved in theater again, although her activities were strictly backstage. She supposed she would stick to being on the crew this year, too, but a small part of her longed to try out for a role in one of the productions. It was a scary thought, but she felt a thrill of anticipation as well. She'd have to see how she felt about it once the play was announced.

The Fine Arts Complex was fairly new, but the smell backstage was the same one she had inhaled in theaters all her life—a mixture of greasepaint, mothballs, and wood shavings. Stepping over some cable, Maddie could tell that being back in the theater had already lifted her spirits.

"Hey, Maddie, how are you?" A short, wiry guy

with a blond crew cut came up and put his arm around Maddie's shoulder.

"Ben!" Delighted, Maddie gave him a kiss on the cheek. "I thought you were going to take a semester off to try your luck in New York."

"I was up there during the summer, and I found a great job—as a waiter. So I decided I ought to hightail it back here and graduate."

"Sounds like a good idea." Maddie laughed.

"Hey, you cut your hair," he said, giving it a little ruffle. "Looks cute, a little like Oliver Twist's."

Maddie tugged at the ends. "I wish it would grow."

"Why?" Ben asked, bewildered.

"Never mind."

As they moved from the backstage area to the front of the theater Maddie asked, "Are you going to be the assistant director again this year?"

Ben smiled proudly. "Sure am. As a matter of fact, Professor Olin has given me a lot more authority. I'm going to practically run the first production."

"Great," Maddie congratulated him. "What's it going to be?"

Ben ran a hand through his short hair. "I'm not sure yet, but I'd love to do a musical."

"Wonderful. There are so many good ones, like *West Side Story*, *My Fair Lady* . . ."

"Yeah, well, it all depends on what kind of talent we pull in this year."

"I suppose there'll be a lot of the same kids—Jane Atkinson, and Tony Moriartry . . ."

"No, Tony was a senior. He's gone. And Jane's transferred to Yale Drama School. There is one new guy on campus who's been over here a couple of times bugging me about try-outs. His name is Mike Genovese."

"Is he any good?"

"I haven't got a clue. He says he can sing and act."

"Some enchanted evening . . ." A warm baritone voice suddenly sounded from behind the curtain.

"What the—?" Ben began looking around.

"You may meet a stranger . . ."

Maddie's eyes opened wide. The handsome boy who had helped her on the bus was strolling onto the stage, still singing. He stopped in front of Maddie. "But you're not a stranger. I saw you on the bus."

Maddie blushed. "That's right."

"How about an introduction, Ben?"

Ben grimaced, but said, "Madison Lerner, this is Mike Genovese."

"Madison? Like the president or like the avenue?"

"Please call me Maddie. Everyone does."

Mike smiled down at her with soft gray eyes. "Maddie it is."

Maddie wracked her brain for something clever or witty to say, but all she could squeak out was, "So where did you transfer from?"

"I went to UCLA for a few semesters, then I worked for a while, acting in commercials."

"Really? Have I seen you in any?"

"Well, a couple of years ago I was one of the kids on the beach having a great time downing some orange juice. The last one I did was a laundry commercial. My mother couldn't get my socks clean enough."

Ben interrupted their laughter. "Hey, I'd like to hang around and discuss your credits all afternoon, Mike, but I wasn't done talking to Maddie."

Mike backed away, his hands up in a gesture of compliance. "Sure. Sorry I butted in. See you around, Maddie. Bye, Ben."

As soon as Mike was out of earshot, Maddie asked, "Why did you do that?"

Ben looked embarrassed. "Well, we weren't done talking, were we?"

"I don't know, but that was no reason to tell the guy to get lost."

"He looked interested," Ben said belligerently.

"So? What if he was?"

"Maddie, he's not for you." Ben raised his head and looked directly into her eyes. "Really."

Maddie shook her head. "You're crazy. A guy I've barely met says two words to me, and you think you have to protect me from him?"

"Look, I'm sorry. I guess I was interfering."

"I guess you were," Maddie said tartly. Then she softened when she saw Ben's hurt look. "Oh, never mind. If I join the theater crew I'll see him around."

Maddie saw him sooner than that. After Ben gave her a tour of the building's new lighting and sound system, Maddie left to go back to the dorm. She practically tripped over Mike, who was lounging on the stone steps outside.

"Well, hello again," he said, looking up at her, shading his eyes from the bright sun with his hand.

"Hi," Maddie said shyly.

"Ready to go?" Mike stood up quickly.

"Weren't you waiting for someone?" Maddie asked, confused.

"Sure I was. You. You didn't think I was going to let Ben scare me off, did you?"

Maddie just stood there. She was so surprised, she didn't think she could move.

"You're not dating Ben, are you?" he asked.

Ben was great, but hardly the sort Maddie was attracted to. "No, we're just friends."

Mike gently put his hand on Maddie's shoulder and led her down the stairs. "Good. I hope we'll be friends, too."

Maddie could hardly believe her luck. Mike Genovese was one of the best-looking guys she had ever seen, and he actually seemed interested in her, Madison Lerner. A tight little knot in the pit of her stomach reminded her that she'd hardly said a word. If she was going to keep a guy like Mike interested, she would have to do better.

"So, how did you wind up in the middle of Georgia after living in L.A?" Maddie asked. It wasn't exactly sparkling repartee, but at least it was a conversation opener.

"Well, I couldn't get any work and then I got to the point where I wasn't even going out for auditions. So I decided I should go back to school and find something else to do in case the acting thing doesn't work out," Mike answered.

"But that still doesn't explain how you wound up at Hawthorne," Maddie pointed out.

"True. Well, for one thing, they accepted me. For another, my grandparents live outside of Atlanta, so I'll be near family."

"That's funny, I have a great-aunt who lives nearby, too. She's been so good to me since I've been here—I even lived with her for a few weeks. You're right, it is nice to be close to family."

"Yeah, at least I can get a home-cooked meal every once in a while. From what I've tasted at the Commons dining room, I'm going to need it."

Maddie barely heard Mike's last comment. She was all too aware that the guy she was walking next to was a "major hunk," as her old roommates would put it. If she needed any proof, it was the way the female population walking by stared at him with frank interest. As Maddie and Mike rounded the corner of the science building, they passed Erica, who raised her eyebrows a bit, obviously surprised to see Maddie with such a sophisticated, handsome boy. But Mike was moving at such a fast clip, it was all Maddie could do to keep up with him, much less stop for an introduction.

"Are you going to try out for some of the productions?" Maddie asked, still trying to make conversation. "Ben mentioned that you might."

"Oh, sure. I always want to keep my hand in the world of the theater." He emphasized the last phrase with a very heavy, fake British accent, and Maddie giggled. "How about you, luv?" he asked.

"I . . . uh . . . I don't think so," Maddie faltered. "I'm used to being behind the scenes." The thought of co-starring with Mike in the fall musical was a tantalizing one. It would be fun to take a leading role opposite him—particularly in a play that had plenty of romantic scenes.

All too soon they were in front of Rogers House. "I should be getting in," Maddie said reluctantly. "I already have a psych quiz to study for."

"Okay. I'll see you around." He gave her another one of his dazzling smiles and turned away.

Maddie couldn't help feeling disappointed by Mike's casual good-bye. But what had she expected? That he would hang out with her all afternoon? What made her think for even a second that she could capture the attention of someone like Mike? Unhappily, she turned to walk in the door.

"Maddie?"

Her heart pounded in response to the sound of Mike's voice. "Yes?" she asked as she turned back around to face him.

"I don't know what there is to do around here, but would you like to go to a movie on Saturday night?"

Maddie tried to keep her voice calm. "Saturday? Sure. That would be great."

"Okay, I'll give you a call, and we can set up a time."

Maddie walked slowly up the stairs of Rogers to the third floor; it felt as if she were walking on air. Even Jean noticed her blissful expression when she walked inside the suite.

"You're looking pretty happy," Jean commented. Outfitted in gym shorts and a loose-fitting T-shirt, she looked stronger than ever.

"I am happy," Maddie admitted, dropping into one of the new plush chairs. "I just got asked out by one of the best-looking guys on campus."

Jean gave a low whistle. "You've got to look out for that type."

Stacy walked out of the bedroom, book in hand. "What's this I hear about you and some guy?"

Before Maddie could launch into a description, Erica entered through the front door and unceremoniously dumped her books on the table. "Maddie, who was that boy I saw you with?"

"Is this all over campus already?" Stacy asked, pulling up a chair.

Maddie chuckled. "No, Erica just saw me with this guy I met at the theater group. His name is Mike Genovese, and he asked me to go to the movies with him."

"Fast work," Stacy said. "What's he like?"

"Gorgeous," Erica answered for her.

"He used to be an actor. In commercials, anyway. He's from L.A., and he's going to try out for some of the theater group productions."

Stacy gave her the thumbs-up sign. "Sounds terrific."

"It is." But suddenly Maddie's excitement waned. "I don't know what he wants with *me*."

"That's not a winner's attitude," Jean objected.

Maddie should have known Jean would put everything into a sports motif. "I guess not, but it's an honest one."

"Maddie, you're cute and bright and nice. There's no reason why any guy on campus wouldn't want to date you," Stacy replied staunchly.

"I guess," Maddie said, but her voice was full of uncertainty.

"Well, you'll find out soon enough if the two of you get along," Erica said. She went to the small refrigerator and pulled out a pitcher of iced tea.

"Uh-huh." Even though she agreed with Erica, Maddie wished the girl had been as encouraging as Jean and Stacy.

Erica brought a glass of iced tea to her perfectly colored lips and took a sip. "Were you in the theater group last year, too, Maddie?" she asked.

"I was on the stage crew."

"Oh, you did a lot more than that," Stacy interjected. "You kept the whole show together."

Erica took tiny, graceful steps over to the armchair opposite Maddie, where she sat down and crossed her legs—like a lady, Roni's parents would say. "You know, I was involved in a little Off-Off-Broadway theater group when I was in high school. I was really hoping to become part of the drama club while I was down here."

"You'd probably enjoy it. It's a good group."

"Do you think you could get me in?" Erica asked hopefully.

"I don't really have to get you in," Maddie said. "The theater club is always looking for volunteers."

"To work backstage you mean?"

"Well, yes. Of course, they also hold auditions for the plays. Is that what you want to do, act?"

Erica's eyes grew wide. "Oh, I don't think I'd have the nerve to try out."

"I know the feeling. Look, the next time there's a crew meeting, come with me. I'll introduce you to everyone."

"*Would* you, Maddie?" Erica asked gratefully. "That would really be a help."

"You know," Stacy said, "speaking of activities, as your big sister I should tell both of you what kinds of things are available on campus."

Jean waved her hand. "Nothing extracurricular for me. I've got to concentrate on basketball."

"What about you, Erica? Besides theater, I mean."

"Gee, I don't know. I don't want to load myself down with too much."

Maddie remembered all too clearly the trouble she had gotten into last semester when she had done just that. "You're right," she said approvingly. "Just stick to the stuff you really like."

"Actually, there is one other thing I'd like to know more about," Erica began slowly.

"What's that?" Stacy inquired.

"Well, I always assumed I'd join a sorority in college."

"That shouldn't be a problem," Maddie said, "There are several here on campus."

"Maddie and I belong to Alpha Pi Alpha," Stacy said.

"Alpha Pi?" Erica said enthusiastically. "I hear that's the best house at Hawthorne."

"It's got us, hasn't it?" Stacy agreed.

"During rush week you can visit all the houses," Maddie said quickly. She didn't want Erica to think that she had to go out for Alpha Pi if she liked one of the other sororities better.

"I know, but doesn't the panhellenic board ask you to list your choices?"

"That's right, then they match you with the house that wants you," Stacy explained.

"And it probably helps if some of the sisters put in a good word for you."

"Of course," Stacy said, looking at Erica a little curiously. "But Maddie's right. You probably shouldn't set your heart on one house until you get a chance to see them all."

"Oh, I agree totally," Erica said, "but I know I would just love it over at Alpha Pi. I mean, if the other girls are anything like you two."

Maddie glowed a little inside. It felt good being a big sister and being able to show Erica the ropes. And it would be great being her sorority sister if that worked out. Then, of course, there was Mike. To meet a guy like him during the first week of school and to actually have a date with him. . . Maddie sat back in her chair. This was turning out to be a really great year after all.

Chapter 4

Roni looked at herself in the bathroom mirror. She supposed, objectively, she would be called pretty. Wavy auburn hair, catlike green eyes and just a sprinkle of freckles across the bridge of her turned-up nose. But she didn't feel pretty. She turned away from the mirror with a sigh. If she felt anything, it was depressed.

She flopped down on her bed, not caring that she was wrinkling the emerald-green t-shirt dress she had bought only that afternoon. It was on her way home from Whiz!, the only decent clothes store in Hawthorne Springs, that she had run into Zack. It was the first time she had seen him since she'd come back to campus. She knew it had to happen sometime: Hawthorne was just too small to avoid people permanently.

Still, if she had to see him, Roni wished she could have been on the arm of some good-looking guy. Instead, it was Zack who had been holding hands with a petite blond girl as they wandered down Main Street. There had been a moment of awkward hellos, then they moved on. When Roni looked cautiously over her shoulder, she could see the girl whispering in Zack's ear.

Roni wasn't sure what had gone wrong between her and Zack. She supposed the relationship had just run its course, but Zack was one of the nicest guys she had ever dated and she had a feeling she would never find someone as sweet as he was again. The party she had gone to last night had proved that. There were half as many boys as girls, and the ones who did show up were mostly freshmen—boring freshmen.

Roni grabbed the little calico cat that sat on the end table next to her bed. Zack had given it to her at the end of the spring semester, saying the feline's wicked little smile reminded him of Roni. But the best thing about Zack was that although he could see the wickedness and wildness in her, he always made Roni feel peaceful.

Before she met Zack, being zany and unpredictable were Roni's trademarks. There wasn't a party she wouldn't go to, or laugh she wouldn't have. Thinking back, she realized that some of the fun had only seemed so hilarious because drinking had improved what was actually going on. However, since cracking up Stacy's car last semester, and with the help of Zack, Roni had stopped drinking. But there was no denying she still felt the powerful urge to drink sometimes. She felt that way right now.

Stretched out on the bed, Roni could feel herself getting sleepy. She was accustomed to the suffocating Georgia heat, but sometimes it just seemed overpowering. Of course, she could get up and turn on the air conditioner, but even that seemed like a major undertaking. She turned toward the open bedroom door and hoped a breeze would come her way.

She was almost asleep when she heard the front door to the suite shut with a bang. "Anybody home?" Liz called, but Roni was too tired to answer.

"I guess neither of our sophomore roomies is around," Roni heard Angie say.

"How do you think it's going?" Liz asked as she kicked off her shoes and settled into a chair. "I mean, the suite and all."

"I think Sam is nice enough," Angie replied, her voice barely audible.

"And Roni?"

"I'm not so sure about Roni." Angie popped open a can of apple juice and slammed the refrigerator door shut.

"Neither am I," Liz said slowly.

"Have you seen her even open a book?"

"No, and that bothers me. She's always asking if she can turn on the TV or the stereo."

"She even does that when I'm trying to meditate," Angie complained. "And I usually wind up taking my books and going down to the study lounge when I'd rather stay up here."

"I do the same thing," Liz said.

Angie took a long sip of juice. "Do you think we should ask Sam to talk to her?"

"Hmmm, I don't know. They're really good friends. It might put Sam in an awkward position."

"I guess so. Also, we don't want to be crybabies this early in the semester."

"That's true," Liz agreed.

"On the other hand, maybe we should say something. Roni doesn't seem very happy, and she's not doing much for my mood either. Maybe there's something we can do for her."

They kept talking, but Roni didn't want to hear any more. She stuck her fingers in her ears so she could drown out the sound of their voices, afraid that if she shut the door, Liz and Angie would realize that she'd listened to their entire conversation. *How dare they*, she thought. *Who are they to sit around and feel sorry for her? And to ask Sam to talk to her? That was all she needed. It would take about a minute for Sam to run to Stacy and Maddie and pretty soon they'd all be giving her advice about pulling herself out of her funk. Why not just tell everyone in Rogers House? Then she could have the pity of a hundred girls. Well, that wasn't going to happen,* she vowed. *She was not going to sit around feeling sorry for herself, wishing her life were different. If there was one thing Roni Davies knew how to do, it was how to have a good time—and she was determined to do just that. She'd show those freshmen a thing or two. She'd show them all.*

When Roni awoke, it was still light outside, but just barely. She squinted her eyes at the glowing red digital clock: seven o'clock. She had missed dinner. Pulling herself out of bed, Roni went into the bathroom and ran a comb through her hair. Her new dress looked like a crumpled sheet, so she shucked it off and pulled a lush flower-print sundress over her head.

Roni wandered out to the living room. It was empty, but she caught sight of Sam reading in the fading light out on the balcony. She walked to the open french doors. "Am I interrupting, or do you want some company?"

Sam put down her book. "Sure"—she motioned—"come on out. I was trying to get through this chemistry, but its not making much sense to me. I think I need a break from all these elements and compounds."

Roni fanned herself as she sat down. "It's still so hot out."

Sam pointed to the bun she had made of her heavy, wheat-colored hair. "I know. Maybe I should have my hair cut like Maddie's."

Maddie had come over last night to tell them about her upcoming date with Mike Genovese.

Roni had tried to be happy for her, but the idea of Maddie Lerner going out with some movie star made her feel even worse about her own single condition. "Your hair looks just fine the way it is," she said lifelessly. "I wouldn't cut it."

Sam peered at Roni more closely. "Not exactly an enthusiastic compliment. I've been meaning to ask you if something's wrong, Roni. You really haven't been yourself since school started."

"Have you been talking to Liz and Angie?" Roni flared.

Sam seemed honestly surprised. "About what?"

"They were in the living room this afternoon commiserating about what a rotten roommate I am. Always moping around, wanting to listen to loud music on the stereo."

"Well," Sam said thoughtfully, "you know they're just starting out. They probably want to make sure they get all their studying done. You remember how we were last year—especially Terry. They're just nervous."

"But the room's a tomb," Roni complained.

Sam cracked a small smile. "Hey, I'm sorry the three of us seem like a drag, but you should let it be a good influence on you, Roni. I don't think you've opened a book since you've been here."

"You're keeping kind of close tabs on me, aren't you?" Roni bristled.

"Cool it, Roni. All I'm saying is that you can't really put down Liz and Angie for wanting a good study environment. And if you want to be miserable by yourself, that's your business."

Sam obviously meant this last remark to be conciliatory, but to Roni it just seemed plain condescending. "Oh, so you think I'm just dragging around ruining everyone's day, is that it?"

Sam threw up her hands. "No, no, you're taking this all wrong. Everyone gets in a bad mood once in a while."

"Mine is just lasting a little too long for everyone's taste, is that it?"

Sam lifted her damp bangs off her forehead. "I'm not going to fight with you, Roni. This is ridiculous."

Roni stood up, her green eyes flashing. "So now I'm ridiculous."

"I didn't say that. . . ."

But before Sam could finish, Roni stormed off the patio into their bedroom and slammed the door behind her. "Fine," she muttered, "if that's the way they want to be." She went over to her large makeup bag in the bathroom and began brushing on some eyeshadow. She chose a sparkling sea green that matched her eyes. Then she carefully outlined the lids with brown pencil, smudging the lines to soften the effect. Her long lashes were transformed with black mascara, and for a finishing touch she put on blusher and then carefully applied lipstick in the same coral color of her dress.

Roni looked at herself with satisfaction. There

was no reason someone who looked this good could not get a guy to notice her. She was going out tonight and if her roommates didn't like it, that was too bad.

"Where are you going?" Sam asked as Roni flew past her.

"To have some fun for a change." By the time she got to the parking lot, Roni felt as free as a bird—like a prisoner who was out on parole. She hummed a tune as she unlocked the MG, then she turned and saw Stacy walking across the parking lot.

Stacy came over to her. "Hey, Roni, you're looking good."

"Thanks. Where are you headed?"

"I'm going to pick up Pete, and we're driving out to see his family. I haven't seen them since I've been back. Mrs. Young promised us some homemade pie. I'd invite you along, but it looks like you have plans," Stacy answered, her curiosity plain.

"That's right." Roni was not about to divulge anything.

"A date?"

"Nope, but I'm going to find one." Without waiting for an answer, Roni hopped in the car and started up the motor.

Stacy placed her hand on the steering wheel. "You're not going to do something crazy, are you?"

"Not you, too," Roni groaned.

"So you *are* up to something. Where are you going?"

"I don't have to tell you. You're not my mother, Stacy. Neither is Sam, and Liz and Angie sure aren't. I'm just going out to have a good time for a change. Not all of us enjoy sitting around a farmhouse eating pie."

Stacy looked shocked by Roni's outburst. "Well, if that's the way you feel about it, fine. I just hope drinking isn't part of the evening's entertainment."

Roni felt her flipness start to vanish. "I can take care of myself," she said quietly.

"I hope so," Stacy replied stiffly. "You've come too far to slip back into your old habits."

As Roni sped across the dark country highway, she considered Stacy's comments. *Stacy was right*, she conceded. Roni didn't want to get back into trouble, but she honestly didn't think that would happen. She was sure that if she took a drink or two now, it wouldn't lead to the problems she had had last year.

Anyway, it wasn't really a drink she was looking for tonight. She was on a mission to find people who liked to have fun. Surely it was early enough in the semester to find people who didn't have their noses completely buried in textbooks.

A few minutes later she arrived at the Heidelberg, a local campus hangout. When she went inside the dark bar the place looked empty, but she did spot Lewis Coulter, a guy who had been in her western civ class last year. She slid into the booth across from him. "Hi, Lewis."

"Well, Roni Davies, hello yourself." He looked at her appreciatively.

"What's happening?"

He shrugged. "Not much. I was just having a beer before I hit the library. Do you want one?"

Roni considered. "No thanks," she said, shaking her head. "I'll just have ginger ale."

Lewis signaled the waitress and ordered Roni's soft drink.

"So," she continued, after the waitress hurried away, "do you really have to go to the library?"

"Yeah, my econ professor has already assigned a paper, and I want to get a head start on it."

"I read in the campus paper that they have a band out at Jake's," she said. Jake's was a nearby roadside cafe that Roni and Zack used to frequent. "Wouldn't you rather be dancing than hanging around some stuffy old library? The place isn't even air conditioned."

"You're tempting me, but I really can't." Then Lewis brightened. "You know, they're having a foreign film festival on campus starting tomorrow. Truffaut's *400 Blows* is playing. Maybe you'd like to go."

Roni stared down at the ginger ale the waitress had placed in front of her. She hated foreign films: Reading subtitles was a drag, and besides, they were usually so boring. "Uh, that's not my thing, Lewis. Maybe some other time."

Roni was afraid she had hurt Lewis's feelings, but he said easily, "No problem." Then he began telling her about the volunteer work he had done during the summer at a camp for the handicapped.

Roni drummed her fingers against the wooden table. She had come out for an evening of fun, and all this was doing was making her more depressed. Out of the corner of her eye she saw a familiar figure go by: It was Zack and his new girlfriend heading for a booth in the back.

"Listen, Lewis, I don't want to keep you," Roni said hastily. She pulled a dollar out of her bag to pay for the ginger ale.

Lewis pushed the money back at her. "Hey, I'm not broke yet. I can afford to buy a pretty girl a drink."

The compliment lifted Roni's spirits a little. "Thanks."

As she got up to leave, Lewis said, "We're still going out sometime, right?"

"Oh, sure." But Roni's eyes were on Zack and his date, laughing together in the back booth. They probably spent the whole day together, she decided. Roni quickly left the Heidelberg and headed for her car.

Well, that was not exactly what I'd call fun, she thought, turning on the ignition. *Where to now?* She let the MG drive itself, and soon she found

herself speeding down the back road that led to
Jake's. A rustic place in the middle of a weeping
willow grove, Jake's was home to truckers and
locals as well as the more adventurous kids
from Hawthorne. Even from a mile away she
could see its blinking neon sign which seemed
to promise good times. When she got a little
closer, she could hear music blaring out the
windows.

Roni nodded with satisfaction as she stepped
inside Jake's. Instead of the quiet coolness of the
Heidelberg, this place was hot. Noisy music was
accented with strobe lights flashing from behind
the bandstand. Cigarette smoke clouded the air,
and the crowded room was filled with laughter
and chattering voices. Roni wished there was
someone there she knew, but she didn't see
anyone familiar.

The band was just taking a break as Roni sat
down at an empty table close to the stage. She
tried to put on an indifferent expression to show
that she didn't care she was alone, but she
needn't have worried. Within seconds, two of
the band members were pulling up chairs next
to her.

"Hello, little lady. Mind if we join you?"

Roni shook her head and smiled. *Not bad,* she
thought, looking from one to the other. The guy
who had spoken put his guitar behind his chair
and ran a hand through his long blond hair. The
other one, smaller and quieter, just nodded and
glanced at her with shy eyes.

"I'm Roni Davies," she said with a smile. "And you're . . . ?"

"Well, collectively we're part of the Waves, but my name is Bud," the blond answered, "and this is Danny, our drummer. You come here often?"

"That's kind of a tired line," Roni teased.

"I doubt she does," Danny said seriously. "We've been here for a week and we've never seen her before."

"Now that *is* true," Bud said. He had a strong Southern accent. "Danny here is the brains of the outfit."

"And what are you?" Roni asked.

"Oh, I'm only the best guitar player this side of Atlanta," he answered as he lit a cigarette.

"Modest, too," Roni said with a wry grin.

"No, just honest."

The waitress suddenly appeared out of the dark haze and stood before them. "Whatch y' all want?" she drawled.

Before Roni could reply, Bud said, "Three beers." Roni felt her heart pound a little, but she figured, what the heck. One beer wouldn't hurt her. Besides, she wasn't about to drink a ginger ale in front of these guys. They'd laugh her right out of Jake's.

"Do you live around here?" Danny asked politely.

"Sort of. I go to school at Hawthorne."

"We thought we'd see more of you college

girls," Bud said, blowing a smoke ring. "But so far, it's been mostly local types."

Roni nodded. "Yeah, they're a real studious bunch at Hawthorne. They don't get out much."

"And you don't fit in?" Bud watched her closely.

"Something like that." Roni took a swig of the beer the waitress had just brought and tried not to make a face. It had been so long since she had touched the stuff, she'd forgotten its sour taste.

"You don't *look* like someone who's used to having a good time."

Roni downed a little more of the beer. "Well, you're wrong. I usually have a *very* good time. It's just hard to find one in Hawthorne Springs."

"Maybe I could show you one."

Roni knew how to treat guys like this. "Honey, I don't think I'm about to let you try."

Bud threw back his head and laughed. "Hey, I like girls who are feisty. Don't I, Dan?"

Danny barely looked up from his beer. "Bud, you just plain like girls," he responded.

"That's true. Hey, waitress, another round of beers here!"

Before Roni could protest, the heavyset waitress had brought them all another round and Bud began regaling the table with stories about life on the road as a guitarist. She had to admit Bud was funny, especially when he told her about one rural dive he had played where the band had to use an abandoned chicken coop as their dressing room.

"So, I'd head out on the stage and there'd be all these feathers stuck to my head. I looked like an Indian or something."

The beer was having its effect on Roni as she laughed uproariously. Bud ordered her another one before jumping back on the stage. "Now you sit here and listen to us, girl." He smiled. "You're going to love this."

Maybe it was the glowing feeling she had from the beer, or maybe it was just being out in a big, fun crowd, but in any case, Roni found herself whooping it up and singing along with the band. When Bud held out his hand to her, it seemed like the most natural thing in the world to climb up onstage and start dancing to the Waves' heavy rockabilly beat.

When the set ended, Danny had to help Roni down off the stage and back to her table. She had begun to feel a little woozy.

"Honey, we're done playing music for tonight," Bud said smoothly. "Why don't you and me go for a little ride? You can show me the sights."

"It's too late to see the sights," Roni said, her words slurring a bit. "Besides, there are no sights around here."

Bud held on to her hand tightly. "Now come on, you don't want the party to end now."

A flash of fear sparked through Roni, and she

pulled her hand away. "I've got to get back to my dorm. It's late."

"You shouldn't drive all the way to campus," Danny said, shaking his head.

Roni realized Danny was right: She had had four or five beers, and that was too much for her. "But I have to get back. My roommate will worry," she argued, trying to think clearly.

"I'll drive you back, then," Bud said. "No problem."

Roni bit her lip. Going off in a car with this guy would be a big mistake; she was sober enough to realize that. She turned to Danny. "Would you please drive me home?"

Danny glanced nervously over at Bud. "Uh, sure, if you want me to."

"Well, well. Still waters run deep, Danny." Bud shoved himself away from the table. "Hey, Bud Palmer doesn't go where he ain't wanted. She's all yours," he said in a mean tone to Danny. "Have fun." With that parting comment he stalked angrily away from the table.

Roni didn't want Danny to think she was interested in him. "I just want a ride back to campus, okay? That's all."

"I know," Danny said. "We're staying in town, so I can walk over to the motel once we get you back to college."

She trusted him instinctively, and true to his word, Danny was a perfect gentleman all the way home. When they were nearing campus, he turned to her and said, "You've got to be careful when you're drinking, Roni."

"I know." She sighed. "I haven't had any beer in a long time, and I guess it went right to my head."

"Drinking doesn't really make a good time better—just different. And it can make a bad time worse."

"Mmm," Roni murmured, barely hearing him. She was practically asleep. Rousing herself a little when they got to the campus grounds, she gave him directions to Rogers House. He helped her out of the car, handed her the keys, and with his arm lightly on her shoulder, directed her toward the front door.

"Do you know how to get to your motel from here?" Roni asked. She really felt awful about the long walk he had ahead of him.

He pointed in the general direction of town. "Sure do. It's right down there."

"Okay. Thanks a lot, Danny. Listen, I'm really sorry about this . . . " she mumbled.

"No problem. You take care, now." He patted her shoulder in a fatherly manner.

But as soon as he disappeared down the road, all thoughts of Danny flew out of Roni's mind. Now her biggest problem was getting into the suite and to bed without anyone noticing she'd been drinking—especially Sam. Roni would never hear the end of it.

Chapter 5

Erica tapped her foot impatiently. She had been waiting for Maddie in front of the Student Union for ten minutes. It shouldn't surprise her, she supposed, that sweet little head-in-the-clouds Maddie would be late, but if there was anything she despised, it was being kept waiting.

Normally she would have just gone over to the theater group herself, but to ensure a meeting with Mike Genovese she had to be with Maddie. Besides, she was determined to get into the Alpha Pi Alpha house, and that meant staying on the good side of both Maddie and Stacy.

She had to admit that she was rather impressed with Stacy Swanson. Her background and pedigree put her right into Erica's class, and

Stacy had the added glamour of an ex-politician for a father. Coming from similar lifestyles made it easy for her and Stacy to develop a fast friendship. The only thing Erica couldn't figure out was why Stacy was dating a geek like Pete Young. He was good-looking enough, she supposed, but he was a local, a farmer, for goodness sakes. Personally, she couldn't imagine having the least bit in common with a farmer, and she had no idea what Pete and Stacy found to talk about. They had broken up at the end of the summer, and now they were getting back together again. Erica couldn't see why.

As for Maddie, she was all right in a prissy sort of way, but she was hardly right for an awesome guy like Mike Genovese. It had been a few days since Erica had first laid eyes on him, but it seemed that his brawny Hollywood looks were etched in her memory. Mike had just met Maddie, and they hadn't even had their first date yet, so they couldn't be all that devoted to each other, Erica told herself. She was just going to have to plant herself firmly between them before their relationship got any more serious.

When the big old clock in the Union Tower struck three, Erica looked around, annoyed. Maddie was nowhere in sight, but she did spy Kitty Armstrong strolling along the quad. Erica and Kitty had gone to summer camp together and had once been bunkmates. They hadn't known they'd both be attending Hawthorne, but when they saw each other there had been a happy reunion and each had become the other's best friend.

Kitty spotted Erica and changed direction, hurrying toward her. "I thought you were going to a Drama Club meeting this afternoon," Kitty said in greeting.

"Maddie hasn't shown up yet," Erica said, not bothering to hide her annoyance.

"You can always go over there by yourself."

"No, I'll wait. Maddie's too conscientious to just leave me here."

Suddenly Maddie came running out of the Union. "I'm sorry I'm late," she said, gasping for breath. "I had to help a friend of mine who was having trouble with her Spanish homework."

"That's okay," Erica said sweetly. "I was just telling Kitty here you wouldn't leave me in the lurch."

"That's what she was saying," Kitty agreed.

"Well, we do have until three-thirty," Maddie said glancing up at the tower clock, "but the Fine Arts Complex is all the way across campus so we'd better get going."

"Absolutely. I'll talk to you later," Erica said to Kitty with a wink.

"So, you were helping someone with Spanish," Erica said as they crossed the quad. "That was nice of you."

"I'm not all that good at it," Maddie answered modestly, "but, this girl seemed totally lost, so I thought I'd show her what I could."

"Stacy tells me you're a real brain."

"Not exactly," Maddie said uncomfortably, "but I do study hard."

"Either way, you come up with good grades. Is Mike smart?" Erica asked, casually slipping his name into the conversation.

"I don't know. I've really only seen him a couple of times. Well, here we are," Maddie said. She held the door to the Fine Arts building open for Erica. "Come on, I'll introduce you around."

Just make sure you make one specific introduction, Erica said silently.

The girls headed backstage and almost immediately ran into Ben, who looked harried. "Maddie, I've been waiting for you. I've got some scripts I want you to check out. Who are you?" he asked, finally noticing Erica.

"This is my roommate, Erica Martin. Erica, this is Ben Robinson, our assistant director and general head honcho."

"Don't say that in front of Professor Olin."

"He couldn't do it without you," Maddie said loyally.

"And I couldn't do much without *you*. Maddie's the best," he told Erica.

"So I hear."

"What about you? Looking for a job on crew?" Ben asked Erica.

"I think so."

"Okay, why don't you work on those scripts with Maddie? They're in the corner over behind the lighting board. I want you to count them and make sure there are twenty-five. Then just check all the pages and see they're complete."

"Aye, aye," Maddie said agreeably.

What a drag, Erica thought, but to Ben she merely said, "We'll get right on it."

As they walked across the theater, Erica kept her eye out for Mike, but she didn't see him. She and Maddie settled down at a scratched formica table. While she dutifully counted the scripts, she still kept glancing around.

"Oh, *Carousel*!" Maddie exclaimed as she picked up one of the scripts. "Professor Olin decided to do a musical."

"That's about the girl who falls in love with a carnival barker, right?"

"Right. There are some wonderful songs in it."

"Did you go to a lot of theater performances in Chicago while you were growing up?" asked Erica.

"Yeah. What about you? I mean, being so close to Broadway and all, you must have seen some really great shows."

Erice brushed her hair away from her face. "Oh, sure. My father's company was always able to get tickets for their clients, so we could pretty much see whatever we wanted."

"You're really lucky."

Out of the corner of her eye, Erica saw Mike walking by. She tried to keep her voice casual, but it was hard to contain her excitement. "Look, Maddie, there goes Mike."

"I saw him," Maddie said, not lifting her head.

"Don't you want to call him over here?"

"He'll come over eventually if he wants to."

It was all Erica could do to keep her voice level. "You really should show him you're interested, Maddie."

Maddie looked at Erica. "Do you think so?" she asked curiously.

"Of course. You don't want him hanging around with other girls when he could be here with you," Erica pointed out.

Maddie glanced over at the stage. Mike was talking to Ben. She cleared her throat and called, "Mike! Hi!"

Mike waved to her and started walking in the girls' direction.

"Now what?" Maddie asked Erica, going into a panic.

"Why . . . just tell him you wanted to introduce him to me," Erica suggested.

Mike stopped in front of their table. There was something about his presence that made Erica shiver.

"Mike, I hope I didn't interrupt you," Maddie said nervously.

"Nah, Ben was just filling me in on the tryouts for *Carousel*."

"I wanted you to meet Erica. She's one of my roommates, and she's going to be on the crew."

Erica could feel herself shaking inside as Mike turned his heart-melting smile in her direction. "Hello, Mike." Her tone was demure, but she gazed into his gray eyes longingly.

"Nice to meet you," he said politely. Then he turned back to Maddie. "Maddie, I wanted to ask you about tomorrow night. What time should I pick you up?"

"Are we going to the Granada?" she asked, mentioning the name of the only theater in Hawthorne Springs.

"Yeah, there's a new comedy there that got pretty good reviews. It starts at eight. We're walking, I'm afraid," he said offering a rueful grin. "I don't have a car."

"That's okay," Maddie said sincerely. "I can use the exercise. Why don't you come by around seven-thirty? That'll give us plenty of time."

"Sounds good," Mike agreed.

"Maddie," Ben's voice called from across the stage. "Can you come here for a second?"

Maddie lifted the scripts off her lap and put them back on the table. "The director calls." Maddie shrugged. "I'll see you later."

Erica was relieved. If she had to listen to any more of Maddie and Mike making plans for their date, she would have gone crazy. Mike seemed as if he was about to turn away, too, but she wasn't about to let that happen. As long as he was standing next to her, she was going to make sure he stayed there a little bit longer. "So, Mike," she began, "Maddie tells me you used to live in L.A. You worked in the industry, didn't you?"

"The industry? That's kind of a pretentious term."

Erica bristled, but she tried to keep her voice pleasant. "That's what my father calls it."

"Oh, is he in *the industry*?"

"As a matter of fact, he owns C & C Advertising Agency." Erica was happy to see that Mike was more than a little impressed by that.

"C & C is one of the biggest in the business."

"Actually, he's not an advertising man. He's CEO of the holding company. But he does like to keep his hand in: He says it's the only one of his companies that he thinks is fun."

"Maybe the business is fun in his position. But being a lowly extra in commercials wasn't quite as amusing."

For some reason the conversation wasn't going very well. Erica decided to try harder. "I'm sure you weren't *always* going to be an extra."

"I didn't think so, either, but I wasn't getting hired, so I decided to go back to school."

"And now you're going to try out for the lead in *Carousel*," Erica said, batting her eyes at him.

"Yeah, probably. What about you? Trying out?"

"I . . . I haven't decided yet."

Mike cocked his head and looked carefully at Erica. "You'd make a cute Julie Jordan."

Erica wasn't sure who Julie was, but she liked being called cute by Mike. Now she was getting somewhere. "Julie Jordan?"

"She's the female lead. Of course, you have to be able to sing."

Deciding not to play her hand yet, Erica

simply said, "I can sing. Whether or not I'd be good enough for a role—any role—we'll have to see."

"Finished with those scripts, Erica?" Ben inquired, coming up behind her.

"Just about."

"Mike, why don't you grab one and we can go over a few things," Ben said. "I have a feeling you're going to be my leading man, so we might as well get some of this nailed down."

"Sure thing." Mike picked up the script Erica handed him, and she could tell his mind was on the play now. She might as well be invisible.

As soon as Mike and Ben were out of sight, Erica picked up her books and headed out the back door. She was sure that Mike would be tied up for the rest of the afternoon, and she had no intention of doing drudge backstage work on the off-chance she might see him again. If Maddie asked what happened to her, Erica planned to say she had gotten a headache and had gone home.

Erica figured it would be awhile before Maddie noticed she was missing so she stopped in the Union grill to get something to drink. After buying a large soda, Erica was thrilled to see Kitty sitting by herself at a table near the door.

"Done already?" Kitty asked with surprise when Erica put her tray down.

"For now. I talked to Mike. He's better-looking close-up than he is from far away, if you can believe it."

"Did he seem interested?" Kitty asked eagerly. She had been hearing about Mike from the moment Erica had first seen him and she knew all the details of Erica's crush.

Erica took a long sip of her Coke. "Mmm . . . I think so. Anyway, it doesn't matter if he's interested. I've decided I'm going to have him, so he doesn't have much of a choice."

"Hey, I give you credit for your ability to attract boys, but what do you mean, 'he doesn't have a choice?' How can you say that when he's already interested in someone else?"

Erica's eyes grew dark and cloudy. "You don't know me all that well, Kitty. I usually get what I want."

"Really?" she said.

"Yes, really," Erica answered, serious. "Besides, I have a plan."

Chapter 6

Maddie whirled around the bedroom like a tornado: She threw clothes all over her bed and then arranged and rearranged the makeup on her dresser. She had thought she was handling her upcoming date with Mike pretty well, but now that he was due to arrive in an hour, Maddie realized just how much this evening meant to her.

"What's all this?" Stacy asked as she came into the room.

"Stacy, where have you been?" Maddie moaned.

"At dinner. I looked all over for you."

"I'm too nervous to eat. My stomach's tied up in knots as it is. I don't think the cafeteria's meat loaf would have helped any."

"Do you want some help getting ready?" Stacy asked.

"Do I ever! Tell me what to wear, and how much makeup to put on. Oh yeah, and tell me how to act and give me a list of topics to talk about."

"Be serious." Stacy laughed. "You've been on dates before."

"Yeah, but never with anyone like Mike Genovese. The more I see him, the less I can figure out why he's going on a date with me."

Stacy patted the bed and motioned for Maddie to come sit beside her. "Listen to me, Madison Lerner. You're smart, pretty, and nice. This guy's lucky you're going out with him."

"Uh-uh," Maddie mumbled, thoroughly unconvinced. Mike was probably used to sophisticated California girls. She felt hopelessly provincial. She glanced over at her clothes, which proved her point.

Stacy followed her gaze. "Let me go through some of these things, and we'll find a great outfit for you."

After Stacy stood up, Maddie stretched out on the bed and moved the clothes into a heap to make more room for herself. "Talk to me, Stacy. Distract me. Tell me about your day."

Stacy held up a yellow blouse and looked at it critically. "Well, I do have some news, but it isn't about me."

"Oh? Who, then?"

"Roni. I saw Sam at dinner. She thinks Roni is drinking again."

Maddie sat upright. "You're kidding!" Maddie hadn't really known Roni when her drinking was a problem, but she'd heard plenty of stories about it.

"Apparently Roni's been complaining about how boring things are, and she also doesn't get along very well with Liz or Angie. Sam was almost asleep the other night when Roni came home. It was late, and she could tell by the way Roni was staggering around that something wasn't right. The next morning Sam asked her where she'd been, and Roni just clammed up."

"What do you think we should do?" Maddie asked with concern.

"I want to talk to her, but I'm going to wait until the right moment. Sam says she's been awfully touchy lately, and I've experienced a little of that myself."

Maddie had learned last semester just how prickly Roni could be when things weren't going her way. "I'll try to talk to her, too, but you're right. If she thinks we're ganging up on her, she's going to be really mad."

Stacy continued sorting Maddie's clothes into two piles. "There," she said putting a peach cotton sweater on top of the larger stack. "I've divided things into two piles: 'possibilities' and 'hopeless.'"

Maddie gestured towards the larger pile. "That's 'hopeless,' I assume."

"I'm afraid so."

Maddie dragged herself off the bed and began

looking through the acceptable pile. "Old, old and boring," she said, quickly dismissing the first three items she looked at. She grabbed a pink skirt from the bottom of the pile. "You think *this* would work?"

"It looks cute on you," Stacy said.

"I've had this since I was a junior in high school. We've got to do better than this."

"All right, then, this calls for serious measures—like raiding my closet."

"Stacy, you're at least four inches taller than I am."

Stacy didn't listen to Maddie's complaint. Instead, she pulled Maddie over to her own closet and started rifling through it. "Let's see, you're only going to the movies. What about this?" She pulled out a slim black linen skirt that looked brand new.

"It's lovely," Maddie said, touching the delicate material.

"It comes to just below my knees, but a skirt like this can be worn long, too. Try it on. As a matter of fact, here's the blouse I bought to wear with it." She drew a white silk blouse out of the closet.

"Stacy, you haven't even worn these yet, the tags are still attached." Maddie's eye was caught by the price on the tags, and her eyes widened. "And these are way too expensive for me to borrow. I might ruin them."

Stacy shook her head. "Forget it. You know me and my limitless clothes budget. If you like the outfit and it looks nice, that'll be good enough for me."

Maddie tried on the clothes carefully. They were a far cry from the casual garb she usually wore, but there was no denying they looked wonderful on her. Maddie posed playfully in front of the mirror.

"You look fabulous. It's a whole new look," Stacy said approvingly. "Now let's see what we can do about makeup."

Maddie approached her dresser with trepidation. She wasn't very confident about applying makeup. Either it looked too heavy or she put it on so lightly that you couldn't even see the difference.

Stacy dragged a white, straightbacked chair over to the bureau. "Sit," she ordered. "I'll take care of this."

Fifteen minutes later Maddie didn't recognize the face in the mirror staring back at her. Her blue eyes looked huge, and instead of her usual pale complexion, her skin was all peaches and cream. "I love it!" she exclaimed. "How did you do it?"

"I'll give you a lesson tomorrow. Pretty soon you'll be able to do it yourself."

"Oh no! Look at the time," Maddie squealed. "Mike'll be here any minute." She rushed around the room and threw a lipstick, some Kleenex, and her keys into a small black purse. By the time she was finished, Jean was knocking on the door announcing that Mike had arrived.

Maddie moved hesitantly into the living room, but whatever qualms she had were calmed by Mike's low whistle. "You look terrific," he said with frank admiration.

"Thank you," Maddie answered shyly.

Stacy stood by, beaming like a proud parent. After a round of introductions, Mike whisked Maddie downstairs. "It was nice meeting your roommates, but I couldn't wait to get you alone," he whispered.

Maddie thought she had died and gone to heaven. She cast a sidelong glance in Mike's direction. In his tight polo shirt, his well-developed muscles were very noticeable. Was there any chance he'd put those strong arms around her? She tried to put the thought out of her mind and focus on what Mike was saying.

"At least it's cooled down a little. Even walking as far as town would have been a drag in the kind of weather we've been having."

"Get used to it," Maddie advised. "It stays warm until Christmas and starts heating up again in March."

"And I thought L.A. could get hot."

"Tell me about Los Angeles," Maddie asked, curious. "Did you live there all your life?"

Mike shook his head. "I was born in a little town between San Francisco and L.A. My parents split up when I was about three, and my mom thought a good way to add some cash to the meager family coffers would be getting me on TV, so we moved to Los Angeles."

"Really?" Maddie couldn't imagine her mother doing anything like that no matter how bad their financial situation became. "How did you feel about that?"

"Me? I was three. All I knew was that every time I got a commercial my mother was really happy, so I tried my best to keep getting jobs."

"That must have been hard for you," Maddie said softly.

"It was, especially since everything in show business is so arbitrary."

"How do you mean?"

"Oh, a kid gets turned down for a part because his hair's the wrong color or he doesn't look good next to an actor who's already been cast. But when you're young you don't understand that. All you hear is a big *no,* and you think something is wrong with you."

"It sounds awful. How long did you do it?" Maddie asked.

"Well, nature kind of tripped me up when I was eight or so. I got ugly."

"You, ugly? I can't believe it." Maddie could have bitten her tongue: What a totally uncool thing to say. But Mike didn't seem surprised by the comment. *Why should he be?* Maddie said to herself. *If he's looked in the mirror lately, he knows he's cute.*

"It's true," Mike continued. "I was skinny, and I had buck teeth. The casting directors told my mother not to bring me in at all anymore."

"That sounds pretty upsetting."

"Not really. I was kind of glad the whole thing was over. Of course my mother didn't exactly feel the same way. I had been bringing home a lot of money; when I stopped getting work, she had to work twice as hard."

Maddie was silent for a moment. This was all such personal stuff that she didn't know what to say to Mike. Still, the story was interesting, and she had to find out the end of it. "But you went back to commercials," she ventured. "You even told me you were trying out for television roles."

"Yep, I went back to it on my own. For one thing I like acting, to say nothing of the money. Then there was the whole star trip. You can't live in Southern California without thinking you might have a shot at the movies or television. I haven't given up that idea, either. I'm taking a break now, but someday I'm going to go back to California and make it big. I swear I am."

Maddie started at Mike's fierce tone. Obviously, his career was something very important to him. "I believe you, Mike."

He smiled down at her. "I appreciate that."

Their engrossing talk had brought them to the edge of town. Mike looked up and down Main Street. "I can't get over how small this place is."

"Hey, Hawthorne Springs is a booming metropolis compared with some of the towns around here."

"I believe it. Where my grandparents live is just a block with a grocery, a gas station, and a post office."

"At least we're not far from Atlanta." Maddie sighed.

"Yeah, I'm looking forward to checking it out. Have you been there?"

"A couple of times."

"Maybe you could show me around."

It was just a casual comment, Maddie knew, but hope rose in her heart: Maybe Mike would see her again.

It was with a heightened sense of expectation that Maddie entered the theater. Just the thought of being alone with Mike in the chilly darkness made her shake. They laughed through the comedy and ate popcorn out of the same large container, but it wasn't until the movie was almost over that Mike whispered something in her ear. When she turned toward him, he cupped her chin in his hand and kissed her on the mouth.

Maddie practically floated out into the lobby after the movie. She didn't even notice Erica, who had stopped right in front of her. "Maddie? Maddie. It's me."

"Oh, hi," Maddie answered, when she had finally focused in on her roommate.

"And Mike," Erica smiled at him with barely masked pleasure. "Pretty good movie, huh?"

"Terrific. Especially those special effects." Maddie wanted to make sure Mike knew she'd enjoyed herself.

"The acting was all right, too," Mike added.

"So, where are you two headed?" Erica asked.

Maddie looked at Mike and he shrugged. "To get a hamburger or something. I hear the Burger Place is pretty good," Mike suggested.

"It is and I'm starved," Maddie said. "I missed dinner."

"Well, let's get out of here."

There was an awkward pause as Mike and Maddie both suddenly realized that Erica was standing forlornly in front of them, making no effort to move on.

Maddie felt compelled to ask Erica along. "Do you want to join us, Erica?" *Surely Erica would have the good sense to say no,* thought Maddie.

But instead Erica was smiling brightly at Maddie and Mike. "I'd love to. The thought of going home to that boring dorm was really bringing me down."

Maddie glanced over at Mike, but to her dismay he didn't seem to be taking the prospect of a threesome too badly. They set off in the direction of the Burger Place with Mike and Erica chattering away like old friends. Things were even worse as the three of them ate their hamburgers as Erica regaled the table with anecdotes about the glamorous people who attended the parties her parents gave. Maddie knew she should join in the conversation, but she really couldn't think of much to add. The people who came to her parents' parties were teachers and office workers. Maddie glanced over at Mike. He seemed enthralled by Erica's stories about the lifestyles of the rich and famous. Maddie felt like a hayseed, and a boring one at that.

Finally it was time to leave the restaurant, and since they were all headed toward Rogers House they walked back together. Maddie watched Erica with a mixture of envy and fascination. Her face lit up as she described the trials of taking a math class for the first time since sophomore year in high school. It was not just that she was cute; she had a magnetic personality.

When they arrived at the door of Rogers House, Erica thanked them for letting her tag along and quickly said her good-nights. At least Erica was getting out of the way at this critical moment, Maddie thought with relief.

Left alone with Mike once more, Maddie suddenly felt shy. "I had a really nice time tonight," she said softly.

"I did too. Erica's a cute kid, but next time, let's make it just us."

"Sounds good to me," Maddie said, thrilled that there would be a next time—without Erica.

Mike took her in his arms and gave her a long, lingering kiss. "Good night, Maddie."

Maddie practically floated upstairs. She was hoping to tell Stacy all about her date, but Erica was in the suite alone. She had already changed into shorty pajamas, and with her makeup off, for once she looked like a little kid.

"Maddie," she began in a rush, "I really want to apologize for tonight. I didn't mean to horn in your date, but I was having a major attack of homesickness, and I just couldn't bear the thought of coming back here and staring at the four walls."

Maddie's heart immediately melted, and the little lecture she had planned to give Erica flew out of her head. She could well remember how lonesome she had been when she first came to Hawthorne. "It's all right, Erica. Everything turned out okay. I'll have another chance to be alone with Mike."

"That's good," Erica said in a flat voice. "Did he ask you out again?"

"Yep," Maddie said cheerfully.

"Well, that's great. And next time I promise I'll leave you guys by yourselves."

"Don't worry about it," Maddie said, patting her on the shoulder as she walked past toward her bedroom. "I'm just glad you didn't have to be alone tonight."

Maddie undressed and carefully hung up Stacy's blouse and skirt. For a moment her mind wandered to Erica and how she had almost ruined her date, but then Mike's face popped into her mind, and all thoughts of her roommate evaporated. She pulled down her bedspread, fluffed up her pillow, and climbed into bed. Maddie could hardly wait to fall asleep—she was sure she'd be having sweet dreams tonight.

Chapter 7

Roni dragged her head off the pillow and glanced at the blinking digital clock: eleven-thirty. If she didn't hurry, she'd miss Sunday brunch.

But when she sat up in bed, the thought of food turned her stomach. The inside of her mouth felt like cotton, and her head throbbed consistently, as if it were a ticking clock.

Roni tumbled out of bed and headed for the bathroom. *Now you've done it,* she told herself, *drinking two nights out of three.* Thursday night at Jake's had been bad enough, but she had really gone overboard yesterday.

As she brushed her teeth, she tried to remember all that had happened the night before. It had started out as a lonely Saturday night. Sam had a date with a guy she knew from last year, and even Angie was going out with someone from her philosophy class. Liz had made plans to get pizza with some of the girls from the dorm and had politely asked Roni if she wanted to come along. Roni declined, not bothering to mention that an evening with a bunch of freshmen was worse than a solitary night in front of the TV.

After everyone had left, Roni had sat on the floor mindlessly eating potato chips and watching shapely women in tights and leotards doing aerobics on TV. When the exercise woman had done her final sit-up, Roni forced herself to get up, put on some lipstick, and get out of the dorm. There had to be something to do on this campus.

Roni wandered past the lake and through the deserted quad. Finally, she found herself on the outskirts of Greek town, one of the livelier areas of campus. Sometimes Roni regretted not joining a sorority, but it was something her mother wanted her to do, so she had immediately rejected the idea without really thinking about it.

Roni ended up in front of the Beta house, where she, Stacy, Maddie, and Sam had rented a suite during the summer. Music was blaring out of the windows. Curious, Roni walked toward the door.

"Roni, how you doin'?" Jim Rose, one of the

Betas she had met during the summer, was sitting on the front stoop.

"What's going on in there?" she asked.

"First beer blast of the season."

"You guys are starting early."

"Of course." He laughed. "Why don't you come inside?"

Roni hesitated, the bad memory of her night at Jake's all too fresh in her mind. Then she figured she might as well go in: she had nothing else to do.

The rest of the evening was sort of a blur. She remembered turning down the first beer that was offered to her, but as the night wore on, and people kept pressing drinks on her, she had finally caved in.

Roni recalled dancing with plenty of partners and even kissing one of them, although for the life of her she couldn't remember exactly who. Eventually, she had staggered home around midnight and fallen into bed.

Roni Davies, that's the last evening you're going to spend drinking, she promised herself as she examined her bloodshot eyes in the bathroom mirror. Then again, the evening had been fun. At least as much as she could remember of it.

After a long, hot shower which helped clear her head, Roni slipped into a pair of tight stirrup pants and a halter top. She had about forty-five minutes before she would miss brunch entirely.

She was halfway out the door when the telephone rang.

"Hello?" she said hurriedly.

"Roni, how are you?"

Roni's heart sunk at the sound of her mother's syrupy voice. It was too early in the day to get into an argument with her mother, but unfortunately, that's what their phone calls usually degenerated into. "I'm fine, Mother," she answered noncommittally.

"You haven't called since you got to school," her mother complained. "We were worried about you."

"Well, there's no need to worry. I'm fine. I've just been busy."

"Are you and your friends all settled in?"

Roni twisted the phone cord. "Not exactly. We got split up. I'm living with Sam and two freshmen."

"New girls? What are they like?" Roni could almost see her mother's frown.

"They're fine."

"You're fine, they're fine. Roni, you never tell me a thing!"

"There's nothing to say, Mother. One of my new roommates, Liz, went to Bloomfield."

"Oh, do I know her?"

"I doubt it. She was a scholarship student." As soon as the words slipped out, Roni realized she had made a major mistake. Her mother hated the idea of opening Bloomfield up to scholarship students. She was always saying that they brought down the school's standards.

"I see," Mrs. Davies answered in just the indignant tone Roni expected.

"Liz Armstrong is a very nice and very smart girl," Roni said hotly. She wasn't all *that* crazy about Liz, but she would certainly defend her to her mother.

"I'm sure she is, but that doesn't mean you have to share a suite with her."

"Mother, is there any special reason you called?" Roni asked, hoping to change the subject.

"As a matter of fact, there is. Your father and I are planning a visit to see you next weekend."

Roni tried to keep the panic out of her voice. "Mom, you don't have to do that."

"Of course we don't have to, but I want to see your living accommodations."

Roni didn't know if that meant her room or her roommates, but either way a visit from her parents spelled trouble. "Maybe you could wait until later in the year. . . ."

"Impossible, dear. Our weekends are all booked up until Christmas. Next Saturday is the only possible date we could come. Besides, we want to come down before you get too busy with studying."

Roni's gaze wandered to the huge stack of books on her desk. She hadn't looked at one in depth since the semester started.

"You *have* been studying, haven't you, dear?"

"We haven't had too much to do yet," Roni mumbled.

"Speak up, Roni. You know I hate it when you don't enunciate."

The list of Roni's actions that her mother hated was a long one. "I know, Mother." As usual Mrs. Davies had managed to make Roni feel as though she were still only five years old.

"So, you'll expect us next Saturday." It was a statement, not a question.

"Yes."

"All right then, your father and I will be looking forward to it."

Roni supposed the appropriate response would be "me, too". But all she said was, "Yes, good-bye."

Her headache, which had faded temporarily with the help of two aspirins, was now back in full force. Roni kicked off her shoes and stretched out on the couch.

It was always like this: Her mother wanted some perfect, obedient daughter, the kind of girl she could never be. She glanced at her watch. It wasn't even noon yet, and she wanted a drink. A chill went down her back, and she started as the door opened. "Oh, Liz," she said, sinking back down on the couch. Then she looked at Liz more closely. "Where have you been all dressed up like that?"

"To church."

It occurred to Roni that Liz had gone to

church last Sunday, too. "Do you go often?" she ventured.

"Every Sunday," Liz said. She put down her pink leather purse and settled into a chair.

Roni rubbed her aching head. "That's nice, I suppose."

"Very," Liz said firmly. "How are you doing?"

"I have a headache."

"Too much partying?"

Roni looked at Liz suspiciously. "What are you talking about?"

"I heard you come in late last night," Liz shrugged.

"Well, what if I was out?" Roni asked defiantly. "A person needs to relax after a hard week of studying."

Liz looked at her with what seemed like x-ray vision.

"Okay," Roni admitted, "I didn't do much in the way of hitting the books this week, but I hardly had any assignments."

"What happened to you, Roni? You used to be such a good student."

Roni's eyes widened. "How would you know?"

"I went to your high school, remember? They used to post the honor roll list, and you were always right there at the top. You won some city-wide essay contest, too, and you read it aloud at a school assembly."

Roni got off the couch and started looking for her purse, too nervous to look Liz in the eye. "That was in another lifetime."

"It was only a few years ago," Liz countered.

"Listen, Liz," she flared, "you don't know anything about college, and you don't know anything about me. For your information, one of the reasons people go away to college is to have fun."

"And are you having fun?" Liz asked simply.

"Yes," Roni yelled, grabbing the purse that had tumbled under the couch. "I am having loads of fun." She slammed out of the suite, flushed with anger. Who did Elizabeth Armstrong think she was, telling her how to run her life?

Even though it was close enough to walk, Roni jumped into her car and headed for the Commons. When another driver cut her off accidentally, she leaned out the window and shook her fist at him. She was still steaming mad when she stalked into the busy dining room.

Roni pulled a container of yogurt from a melting pile of ice cubes and put a tired-looking banana on her tray. She made her way into the dining room, looking for a table where she could sit by herself. But before she could find one, Roni heard her name being called and swiveled around. A few feet away, sat Sam, Stacy, and Maddie gesturing at her to come over. Roni didn't feel like talking—or explaining herself—to them, but there was no graceful way she could sit somewhere else. With a resigned sigh, she carried her tray over to their table.

"Good morning, all," she muttered.

"It's afternoon, and how are you feeling?" Sam asked, eyeing her closely.

"What's that supposed to mean?" Roni snapped.

"Look Roni, I'm not going to pretend I don't know," Stacy replied briskly. "Sam said you were drinking again last night."

Roni peeled her banana, wishing her hands would stop shaking. "I didn't even see Sam when I got in."

"No, but she saw you," Maddie said pointedly.

"And she could smell you," Stacy added. "You reeked of beer."

"Thanks a lot, Sam," Roni said cruelly.

"Roni, we want to help you before this gets out of hand," Sam pleaded.

"You haven't forgotten that last semester you wrecked my car while you were driving under the influence, have you?" Stacy prodded.

"Forget? How can I possibly forget when you're always reminding me. And for your information, even if I have had a few drinks, I haven't been behind the wheel of a car once— my own or anyone else's."

Stacy and Sam exchanged glances as if they didn't believe her.

"It's true," she said, loudly enough to have several people at nearby tables turn their heads to look at her.

"That's fine, Roni," Maddie said soothingly, "but you still shouldn't be out drinking. If there's something bothering you, we want to help."

"Is it because you broke up with Zack?" Sam asked. "I mean, I broke up with Aaron, and it hurts, but it hasn't driven me to drink."

"Well, you're perfect, Sam, and I'm not," Roni answered, stabbing viciously at her yogurt.

"Come on, I didn't mean it that way."

"No? You, apparently, can handle your problems just fine. But I'm unhappy, so I take a drink. Doesn't that make you a better person than me?"

Sam looked hurt. "No."

"Of course it doesn't," Maddie interjected. "It just means you have a different way of handling things."

"What do you know about it, Maddie? You're too busy dating a movie star—at least that's what I hear. You certainly haven't had time to come down and talk to me about it."

Maddie pulled back, surprised. "Well, I've been busy."

"I know, you've all been busy. I've barely seen any of you. I'm stuck in a suite with two freshmen who think they're hot stuff, my former boyfriend is dating some gorgeous blonde, and I'm behind in all my classes. Is that trouble enough for you?"

"Roni, we're concerned. We just want to help," Sam said softly.

Roni stood up. "Sorry, but a lecture isn't going to do it. I'm not some charity case. If you want to be my friends, fine; but I don't want your pity and I don't want you on my case," she emphasized. "Now, I think I'm going for a nice, relaxing drive. I promise that if I get thirsty, I'll stick to root beer." With that, she turned and strode out of the room.

When she got back to the car, Roni sat there for a few minutes trying to calm down. She felt terrible about yelling at her friends like that; She knew she was taking her frustrations out on the few people who wanted to help her the most. Knowing that made her feel even worse. Why couldn't everyone just leave her alone?

To relax herself, Roni started the car and began driving down a country lane. The chirping birds and the lush, green trees rustling in the soft Georgia breeze helped a little, but there was a knot in her stomach that wouldn't go away. Finally, she headed back toward town and drove slowly down a deserted Main Street. There, looking in one of the closed shop windows was Bud, the guitarist she had met at Jake's. She didn't particularly want to see him, but while she was stopped at the light, he turned and recognized her.

"Hi ya, Roni," he said, coming over to the car. Now she had to pull over.

"Hello, Bud. Kind of boring here in Hawthorne Springs on a Sunday afternoon, isn't it?"

He flicked his white-blond hair out of his eyes. "You said it, honey. How about we do something to change that?"

"Like what?"

Without waiting for an invitation, Bud

opened the passenger's door and climbed inside the car. "I don't know, go for a ride, maybe."

"I've been for a ride already."

"Then let's drive to Atlanta," he suggested. "There's bound to be something happening there."

Roni thought about the idea for a moment. If she went back to the dorm, she would have to see her friends, and she wasn't exactly ready for that right now. On the other hand, if she drove into Atlanta she could have some fun. She glanced over at Bud. She was a little uneasy about spending the afternoon with a virtual stranger. She hadn't particularly liked him the other night, but maybe Bud deserved a second chance. Looking at him out of the corner of her eye, she thought he seemed normal enough.

"All right," she agreed. "Let's go for a ride."

An hour later they arrived at the outskirts of the city. The ride had been a surprisingly quiet one, at least in terms of conversation. Roni wasn't in the mood to talk, so she had turned the radio up full blast. Every once in a while Bud changed the stations, but for the most part, he seemed content to be silent as well.

"So, here we are in Atlanta," Roni announced. "Where do you want to go?"

"There's a rock club a couple of miles from here that's pretty good."

"They're open this early?" she asked skeptically.

"Honey, this place is cookin' all the time."

Roni shrugged. "Okay, tell me where to go."

Ten minutes later they were pulling up to a restaurant in one of the seedier parts of town. Somehow the dilapidated ambience appealed to Roni's sense of reckless adventure and she willingly followed Bud inside.

Bud had certainly been right about the place. A band in the corner was belting out a heavy metal tune, and the club was full of people drinking and laughing.

Bud pulled Roni over to an empty table and motioned the waitress over. "What do you want to drink?" he asked.

"Just a Coke, please."

"A Coke?" Bud made a face.

She repeated her order firmly to the waitress, then settled down to listen to the band. But half an hour later she started to get a headache from the loud music. "Let's get out of here," she yelled to Bud, trying to make herself heard over the incessant noise.

"I don't want to leave," Bud said, holding up his glass so that the waitress could see he wanted a refill.

Roni's eyes widened with surprise. She wasn't used to such rude behavior from her dates. Well, Bud wasn't a real date: He was a clod, and after she deposited him back in Hawthorne Springs, with any luck she'd never run into him again.

When Bud finally finished his drink, Roni repeated her request to leave.

"You're a spoilsport," Bud said, scowling, but

he threw a few bills on the table and headed toward the door with Roni at his heels.

"So what do you want to do now?" he asked, squinting into the bright sunlight.

"I want to go back to campus. I've got a lot of studying to do," she insisted.

"Studying! Well, I guess you can't miss out on that," Bud hooted. "But if we stayed in Atlanta, I could show you an awesome time."

"You can stay, Bud." Roni prayed he'd take her up on the offer and get out of her life, but when she walked to the car, unfortunately Bud was right behind her. After she got in the car, Roni sighed and unlocked the door on his side.

They were about a half hour out of Atlanta when Bud pulled a small leather pouch from his shirt pocket, along with a packet of cigarette papers.

"What are you doing?" Roni asked sharply.

"Rolling a joint. What did you think I was doing?"

"Right here in the car?"

"Hey, no one's going to see us."

"That's not the point," Roni protested. "I wish you wouldn't."

"Sorry, babe. I really need a hit right now." Bud lit the joint and inhaled deeply, then held out the burning cigarette in her direction. "Are you sure you don't want some?"

Roni shook her head. "No. I mean, yes, I'm sure."

"Come on, try it. It's great stuff."

"I told you, I don't want any," Roni snapped. But being in that enclosed little space with Bud made Roni wonder if she wasn't getting high just from the smoke blowing in her face. She was certainly getting paranoid. She imagined state trooper cars behind every tree and bush. She wanted to go as fast as possible so she could get Bud back to town and out of her car, but she had to keep to the speed limit to avoid calling attention to her car. It was the longest, most tortured drive she had ever taken.

Finally Roni pulled onto a side street in downtown Hawthorne Springs. "We're back," she said curtly.

Bud smiled at her wickedly. His eyes were pink, and he looked as if he was in a daze. "You don't want to end the party now, do you?"

Roni was almost ready to scream, but she tried to keep her cool. "There *is* no party, Bud."

"There could be." With that, he reached over and gave her a short, harsh kiss.

Roni pulled away immediately. "Get out, Bud. Right now," she ordered.

"What?" He looked stunned.

"I said, get out right now or I'll scream for a cop. You wouldn't want that, would you?"

Now Bud's small, bloodshot eyes were filled with fury. "What's with you? First you dump me at Jake's, and now after spending the whole afternoon together, you start acting like you don't want me anywhere near you."

Roni's eyes filled with tears. "Will you please

just leave," she said, trying to keep her voice under control.

Bud hoisted himself out of the small car, but then he poked his head back through the window. "You are one messed-up girl, you know that?"

Roni was relieved when Bud walked away down the street. But as she headed back to campus, she was overcome with self-loathing. Why had she picked up Bud in the first place? And why had she gone all the way to Atlanta with him? She couldn't even blame her behavior on alcohol: She hadn't had a drink all afternoon. Tears formed in Roni's eyes and began falling silently down her cheeks. The very worst part was that no matter how she tried to explain her behavior, there was no explanation. Stupid Bud was right—she was one messed-up girl.

Chapter 8

Maddie couldn't believe how much work the crew had accomplished in just a couple of days. Everywhere she looked there were kids hammering, sawing, and painting. The intricate scenery was really coming into shape. Almost everyone, boys and girls, were dressed in cutoffs and old T-shirts, and those who weren't covered with sawdust sported paint spots on their clothes. Only Erica seemed immune from all the dirt and mess. Maddie didn't know how she managed it, but she suspected the small amount of work that Erica actually performed was a big clue. Glancing in Erica's direction, Maddie had to restrain a laugh. Erica stood there, surrounded by people wielding noisy saws, and she looked as though she was vacationing on a tropical island. Chatting away with a bottle of pop in her hand, she was wearing pink shorts and a pink polka-dot shirt freshly ironed and tied calypso-style at her waist. Her dark hair, piled on top of her head and secured with a pink bow, only added to the cool, calm effect.

Ben had sidled up to Maddie a few minutes ago and whispered, "How does she do it? Does she keep a change of clothes in the wardrobe room, or what?" She had giggled, but at the same time she renewed her resolve to start acting more like Erica.

"Hey, Maddie, come out of it. You look like you're in another world."

Maddie smiled up at Mike. Her first impulse was to blurt out that she was devising a self-improvement plan, but she bit her tongue: Erica would never say anything like that. She had to think fast. "I was in another world, Mike," she said coyly. "I was thinking about our next date."

Mike's eyes widened, then he grinned. "I'm glad to hear that. I can't promise you a trip to the moon, but what about if we skip the Commons tonight and head over to the PizzaRoo?"

"Oh, Mike, I can't tonight," Maddie said, disappointed. "It's the Alpha Pi Alpha rush tea and Stacy and I have to be there."

"You mean you'd rather spend the evening with a bunch of silly pledges?" he joked.

"Hardly. But this is our first big event of the

semester. Besides, we're taking Erica over so we can introduce her to the rest of the girls."

Mike looked over his shoulder at Erica, who was still talking a mile a minute. "You know, I can't figure that one out. Sometimes I think she's completely in control and then she can come across like a timid little girl who needs someone to protect her. You live with Erica. What's she really like?"

Maddie didn't want to talk about Erica, but it was a fair question—one that had been tumbling around in her own mind. "I honestly don't know," she answered.

Later that evening, back in Suite 3A, there was no hint of Erica's helpless-child personality. She had shucked her casual attire and put on a black linen dress, a silver choker, and intricately designed silver earrings. She looked more like a career woman in her mid-twenties than a college freshman.

"You look fabulous," Maddie gasped when Erica came out of her bedroom. Her own pale dress with its puffed sleeves certainly seemed babyish in comparison.

Stacy, who was pouring herself a cup of coffee, looked up. No slouch in the sophistication department herself, she nodded approvingly at Erica. "That's a great dress. I love your earrings." Stacy came over to Erica for a closer look. "Where did you get them?"

"A little place on the Upper West Side. The artist does one-of-a-kind pieces."

Maddie fingered her own blue-and-white ceramic earrings. If she remembered correctly, she had purchased them at a cut-rate clothing outlet where there were dozens of identical pairs thrown in a bin.

"I just love them," Stacy said again. "You'll have to give me the name of the place. My mother has some jewelry pieces in her art gallery, and she may want to get in touch with this artist."

Maddie found this whole conversation irritating. "It's almost seven," she briskly informed her roommates. "Don't you think we ought to get going?"

"Do you want to walk or drive?" Stacy asked. She picked up the red linen blazer that topped her own dress.

"Drive," Maddie and Erica said in unison.

Stacy laughed. "You're right, I suppose. It's hot out there. Even though we could use the exercise," she added.

"I get enough exercise running around backstage," Maddie commented as they closed the door to the suite.

"Me, too," Erica said with a sigh.

Maddie looked over her shoulder to see if Erica was being sarcastic, but she seemed perfectly serious.

The girls were on their way to the parking lot when Maddie caught sight of Liz. She was dressed in a lovely yellow suit. "Hi, Liz," Maddie called to her.

"Hi," Liz answered.

"Can we give you a lift somewhere?" Stacy asked. "We were just saying that it's a hot night to be walking around."

"I'm going to the tea at the Alpha Pi Alpha house," Liz replied.

Maddie couldn't have been more surprised; Liz didn't seem like the type who'd be interested in sorority life. She involuntarily glanced over at Stacy, who seemed equally taken aback. "That's great, Liz," Maddie said. "We're APA's and we're taking Erica over to the tea. Why don't you join us, and we'll introduce you to everyone?"

Liz nodded slowly. "That sounds great."

"I think you'll like the girls," Maddie said as they sped off in the direction of the sorority house. "They're really a nice group."

"I'm surprised you're going out for rush," Erica said conversationally. "Being a scholarship student and all."

Maddie was horrified at Erica's casual comment. She couldn't believe Erica would say something so rude to Liz. It was none of her business how much money Liz did or didn't have.

There was an uncomfortable silence for a few seconds, then, finally, Liz spoke. "I have a full scholarship that includes tuition, and room and board. So I decided to use the money I earned this summer for sorority dues."

"That's nice," Erica said disinterestedly. Obviously, it hadn't occurred to her that she might be embarrassing Liz. Maddie could see Liz in the rearview mirror, folding and refolding her hanky. After that, Maddie tried very hard to keep the conversation light.

Once they were inside the stately Alpha Pi Alpha house, Maddie didn't have to worry about making small talk: There were girls laughing and chatting everywhere in the large living room. There were so many, in fact, that they took up the sedate little sitting room and spilled over into the dining area.

"So many people," Erica said with a tremulous little laugh. "Where should we start?"

"That's why we're here," Stacy answered. "Stick with us, and we'll make sure you meet the right ones."

No sooner had Stacy spoken than the president of APA, Rita Righterman, came up and was introduced. Maddie could tell at a glance she was charmed by Erica, but just the tiniest bit surprised at seeing Liz. As Maddie kept an eye on both girls as they mingled, she saw the same response on several other faces. Most of the girls were perfectly charming to Liz, but there were two or three who had to make a conscious effort to mask the surprise—and in one case the dislike—in their eyes.

Despite this veiled tension, Maddie thought things were going pretty well. It always gave her such a calm feeling to be in this beautifully appointed house, with its traditional wing chairs, flowery print wallpaper, and flowing lace curtains. Maddie supposed it wasn't for the person who liked modern decor, but she was a traditionalist, and it also appealed to her sensible nature.

As Maddie wandered around, greeting the freshmen guests, some nervous, others perfectly at ease, she decided that having to pick and choose among the rushees was the worst part of sorority life. At its best, a sorority was like a sisterhood where you found girls who would be your friends for life. But sororities could also be cliques, where girls who were left out of the exclusive circle were sometimes scarred forever. She hoped Erica and Liz would both make it into APA if that's what they wanted.

With a glass of punch in one hand and balancing a canape filled plate in another, Maddie sidled up to a group of girls talking to Liz.

Alice Chevenson was talking at the moment, and Liz looked extremely uncomfortable. "One of the girls said you were on scholarship."

"That's right," Liz admitted.

"Neat. Did you get it because you're black?"

Maddie almost spilled her punch. Alice wasn't well known for her brains, but this was ridiculous.

"No," Liz said firmly. "I got it because I am smart."

Maddie cheered silently for Liz, and looked menacingly at Alice.

Meg Morrison, one of the seniors in the circle, also gave Alice a dirty look. "That's great, Liz. We really like our pledges to stay on top of their studies."

"That doesn't mean we don't take time for fun," one of the other girls threw in. "We have lots of dances."

"Will that be a problem for you?" Alice asked Liz.

"What do you mean?"

"Well, there aren't that many black guys on campus."

"I'm sure I'll find a few," Liz said hostilely. With that, she turned and walked out on the terrace.

A horrified Maddie put down the plate she had been carrying and hurried after her. Once she was outside, Maddie was grateful they were alone; she would have hated to have this talk in front of an audience. "Liz . . ." she began tentatively.

Liz whirled around. "What is it, Maddie?" she asked coldly.

"Look," Maddie began lamely, "I know Alice is kind of an airhead, but you shouldn't let her get you upset."

"I don't even know her," Liz said, maintaining a level tone. "Why should I be upset?"

"Because what she was saying was stupid, and ignorant. But really, Liz, most of the girls aren't like Alice."

Liz looked at her squarely. "Maybe most of them aren't, but enough of them are."

"Only a couple," Maddie insisted. "And it's just because they don't know better."

Tears welled up in Liz's eyes despite her efforts to remain cool. "I was a fool to think I could join a sorority at this school," she said bitterly.

"You're wrong," Maddie protested. "Most of the girls here like you, I can tell. I know them better than you do."

"Maddie, you don't know anything. You don't know what it's like for people to dislike you just because of the color of your skin. Look, I know you're trying to be nice, but I don't believe your friends are as good-hearted as you are. And I don't feel like sticking around here just to be insulted." With that, she hurried through the patio doors.

Maddie was standing on the patio alone, trying to sort through her thoughts when Stacy joined her. She was upset, too. "What's wrong with Liz?" she asked. "I saw her come out of here near tears."

Maddie shook her head, then briefly recounted the whole story.

"That's awful," Stacy said, obviously appalled by her sorority sisters' behavior.

"I know, but what can we do about it?"

Stacy sat down on one of the patio chairs. "Not much. I mean, what Alice said was really tactless, but I think Liz was overreacting too, and you tried to tell her that."

Maddie pulled up a chair next to Stacy's. "Yes,

but we've got to consider the fact that Liz must go through this all the time. It can't be pleasant. Maybe she's *not* overreacting."

"You're right," Stacy said thoughtfully. "I suppose Liz has gotten those responses year after year, and she just comes to expect them now."

"What a mess," Maddie sighed.

The girls were interrupted by Rita Righterman, who wandered out to the patio. "I hope I'm not bothering you. It's getting to be a little too crowded in there. I need a breath of fresh air."

"No problem—but it's hardly fresh," Maddie said. "It's as muggy as ever."

"Guess what?" Rita said. "Erica is the hit of the evening. All the girls think she's just great. I've heard nothing but positive comments about her."

This didn't exactly surprise Maddie. She was used to Erica's social success. "What about Liz?" she wanted to know.

"The black girl?"

Well, Maddie thought to herself, maybe Liz *was* right. People did identify her with the color of her skin before anything else. She nodded.

"I was really impressed by her. Not only is she smart, she seems very nice," Rita commented.

"So you think APA would pledge her?" Stacy asked.

"I haven't taken a survey or anything, but I can't imagine the other members not feeling the same way I do."

"That's interesting," Stacy said.

"Why?"

"Oh, I just don't think Liz thought the girls liked her."

"I'm sure that's not true," Rita said emphatically.

"I'm glad to hear that," Maddie responded, relief in her voice. She had been thinking that it would be hard for her to stay in a sorority that wouldn't take a girl because of her skin color.

After Rita went back inside, Maddie turned to Stacy. "Are you ready to go home? I've had it. It's been a really long evening."

"We'll have to round up Little Miss Personality, first," Stacy said with a rueful smile. "From the way Rita was talking, it sounds as though Erica has her bid all sewn up."

"It certainly does. You know, Stacy," Maddie began impulsively, "since Erica's been around I've really been giving some thought to my image."

"Your image? What's wrong with your image?" Stacy asked indignantly. "I think it's great. And so does Mike, I might add."

Maddie gave her a crooked grin. "Thanks, but honestly, I would like to get some new clothes and maybe some makeup. My Aunt Fitty just sent me a belated birthday check, and she told me to spend it any way I want. Stacy," Maddie finished in a rush, "will you help me with my make-over?"

Stacy patted Maddie's arm. "I repeat, a make-over is not necessary." Then before Maddie could protest, she added, "However, if you insist, I'll go shopping with you."

Maddie wished she had the confidence in herself that Stacy had. Now that she was dating Mike, she didn't see how she could just keep wearing her little button-down oxford-cloth shirts and plain, boring pants. Mike was sophisticated, and if she wanted to keep his interest, she would have to make a few changes. And with Stacy's help, she was going to do just that.

Chapter 9

"Well," Maddie said, craning her neck to look at Stacy, "what do you think?"

Stacy bit the corner of her lip. "It's a beautiful dress."

"It certainly is," the heavily made-up saleslady put in.

"But do you really think it's you?" Stacy asked.

"Of course it isn't," Maddie said, transfixed by her own image. "That's the point." The sophisticated black cocktail dress was something you would see on a New York model, Maddie thought with satisfaction. All the clothes she had chosen were the same style, and they were mostly black. Maddie never had worn that much black, but she thought sophomore year was definitely a good time to start.

119

Maddie and Stacy had cut their afternoon classes to drive into Atlanta. Maddie felt she'd have a better chance buying the elusive new image she had in mind in a big city.

She hadn't been disappointed. Aunt Fitty's check was generous, and so far Maddie had purchased a daring black sundress, an elegant black-and-white short-sleeved silk shirt, and now this dress. "I'll take it," she told the saleslady.

"Boy, I'm not sure you needed me along for this," Stacy said as they headed toward the parking garage. "You seemed to know just what you wanted."

"I really only knew I wanted something different. Are they too different?" she questioned Stacy.

"I guess there's nothing wrong with wanting to try something new," Stacy said slowly.

"Oh look, Stacy!" Maddie stopped, transfixed in front of a jewelry shop window. "Those silver earrings are fantastic."

"They sure are," Stacy said, following Maddie's gaze, "but I thought you said you just ran out of money."

"I did. However, I do have the charge card my parents gave me for an emergency."

"Are earrings an emergency?" Stacy lifted her eyebrows.

"Well, they're a fashion emergency. You know silver jewelry will look terrific with all the black clothes I just bought. Remember how great silver looked on Erica?" Maddie reminded her.

"Sure, silver looks great with black. But Maddie, I have silver earrings you can borrow anytime."

"I know, and I appreciate it, but I'd like to have a pair of my own." She tugged at Stacy's arm. "Let's just go in and see how much they cost."

Inside the cool, quiet jewelry store, the salesman showed Maddie several pairs of silver earrings. "I'll take these," she said, handing back a pair of large silver triangles. A bit nervous, she dug into her purse and found the credit card.

Stacy shook her head. "What are you going to tell your parents when the"—she plucked one of the store's cards from a silver tray—"the Hudson's Jewelers bill appears on their credit card statement?"

"I haven't decided," Maddie answered crossly. She didn't need Stacy to remind her this shopping venture might have some unpleasant ramifications.

When the earrings were wrapped and safely tucked away in one of Maddie's shopping bags, Stacy asked, "Do you want to grab a bite to eat here, or would you rather head back to campus?"

"Well, I'd love to eat here, but I should be getting back. Erica's going to help me with my audition for *Carousel*."

Stacy stopped in the middle of the busy

sidewalk. "You're trying out for *Carousel*? When did you decide that?"

"Actually, it happened yesterday during rehearsal. I was going over the try-out schedule with Ben and I saw the list of people trying out for the role of Julie Jordan."

"Julie Jordan's the lead, right? The girl who falls in love with Billy, the barker at the carousel?"

"Uh-huh. I knew most of the girls on the list and they weren't all that great."

"And since Mike has the role of Billy sewn up, you thought it would be fun playing opposite him," Stacy finished for her.

"Well, it's fun in the fantasy I keep replaying in my head, but actually getting up on the stage is something else again. Starting with the audition."

"It must be scary to get up in front of a bunch of people and sing," Stacy sympathized.

"Fortunately, the try-outs are closed. It'll just be Professor Olin, Ben, and the music director who make the decision."

"But if you get the part, you're going to be performing in front of the whole school."

"Yeah, that's true."

The girls walked into the dark garage, and Maddie insisted on paying the parking tab since the shopping expedition had been her idea. As they looked around for the car, Stacy asked, "Now how did Erica get involved in all this? Is she an actress?"

"So she says. I guess she took drama lessons and was involved in some kind of theater group in New York. When I said I was auditioning, she offered to help me. I figure I can always use a few suggestions."

"Why don't you get Mike to help you?" Stacy asked curiously. "Wouldn't it be more fun than working with Erica?"

"A lot more," Maddie said with a small smile. "But I don't want him to know I'm trying out. I'd be really embarrassed if I didn't make it."

"I don't know," Stacy said. She maneuvered the car out of the garage and into Atlanta's rush hour traffic. "It just seems like Mike's suggestions would carry more weight than Erica's."

It seemed that way to Maddie, too, that evening as she sat across the couch from Erica with the script in her hand.

Jean, as usual, was out at basketball practice, and Stacy had tactfully retreated to Sam and Roni's room. Maddie had just finished singing Julie's song, "If I Loved You." It had sounded pretty good to her, but Erica was full of ideas for improvement.

"You're singing it way too sweetly," Erica criticized. "Don't you want to liven it up a little?"

"Mmm, I don't know. Julie is an inexperienced factory girl. I don't think she has much confidence in herself."

"But she's not a wimp," Erica sighed. "Really,

Maddie, I think you have to interpret the part with a little more punch."

Her comments were the same after Maddie had run through the dialogue in a few of the scenes. "Not spunky enough, Maddie," she said shaking her head. "After all, this girl is going after the handsomest guy in town. Give her a little *oomph*."

Maddie thought about this for a moment. After all, she was interested in the best-looking boy on the Hawthorne campus, and she was trying to act a little more sophisticated to win him over, so maybe there was some basis for that kind of character interpretation. Then she remembered something. "You know, it's been awhile, Erica, but I saw the movie *Carousel*, and the actress who played her was very sweet."

Erica shrugged. "So? That's exactly what acting is all about: taking a role and making it your own. Why do you think they keep reviving *Hamlet*? Different actors do it different ways."

That made sense, Maddie supposed. "All right, I'll try it your way. You're the one with all the experience."

"Oh, I wouldn't say *that*," Erica responded modestly. "I basically just hung around with a lot of theater people, and I took a few singing lessons. You know, the usual."

"Then I still don't understand why you won't try out," Maddie prodded.

Erica got up and went to the refrigerator.

"Want a Coke or something?" she asked over her shoulder.

"No, thanks. I mean, if you've taken lessons, you must have given recitals and put on plays," Maddie persisted.

Erica dropped a few ice cubes in her drink and brought it back over to the couch. "Well, you see, it's like this, Maddie. The last time I was onstage, I had a really bad attack of stage fright."

"You're kidding."

"No, it was awful. I just froze. I couldn't remember a word of my lines."

"So what did you do?"

"Kind of stumbled around until one of the other actors helped me out. But it was just one of the most embarrassing things I've ever experienced."

Maddie could well imagine the humiliation. She shuddered to think how she'd feel if something like that happened to her.

"So," Erica continued, "I just haven't done much with theater since then. You understand," she said, her eyes downcast.

Maddie felt quilty for even bringing up what was so obviously a painful memory. "Say, would you mind listening to me sing this song one more time?" she asked, changing the subject.

"Of course not. I'll be glad to listen." Erica smiled warmly at Maddie.

Maddie and Erica spent the next hour or so going over the role. Erica made more suggestions that seemed off-base to Maddie, but when Erica explained her reasons for the interpretations, they made sense and she decided to incorporate them into her audition.

When Erica finally pleaded time for studying, Maddie stayed on the couch and reviewed the script until Stacy came in. "Well, hello," Maddie greeted her. "What's the news from down the hall? You certainly stayed long enough."

"I wanted to give the budding actress some time to work on her role. And then I got involved talking to Sam."

"How's she doing? We see each other at mealtimes and that's about it."

"Sam's okay. She's been on a few dates, but she's still trying to get over Aaron. Plus she's studying a lot. You know Sam."

"And Roni?" Maddie asked, putting down her script and giving Stacy her full attention.

Stacy sat down and put her feet up on the coffee table. "It's a weird thing about Roni. Nobody seems to see her. Sam says she sleeps a lot and that's about it. She won't talk much, she just seems kind of depressed. Sam suggested we all go out to dinner sometime, but Roni wasn't interested, I guess."

"You know, the day we went to Atlanta I went down to Roni's room and asked her if she wanted to come with us. If anyone loves shopping expeditions, it's Roni."

"And she didn't want to come?"

"Nope. She said her parents were coming

down this weekend, and she didn't want to be in the same city with them until she absolutely had to."

"That's weird. I mean, I can understand Roni not wanting to take a chance on running into her parents, but that's never really bothered her before."

"She's never been so depressed before. Let's make more of an effort to include her when we do things," Maddie suggested. "Maybe she's feeling left out."

"But she keeps refusing," Stacy pointed out.

"Has she been partying a lot on her own?"

Stacy shook her head. "Sam doesn't think so. At least it doesn't seem like she's been out drinking."

"Well, that's something, anyway." Maddie yawned. "I guess I better get to bed if I want to look decent tomorrow."

"You've got your speech and song nailed down?"

"I hope so," Maddie answered fervently. "Erica gave me a lot of pointers."

"Does she know what she's talking about?" Stacy asked curiously.

"She better. I'm basing my whole interpretation of the part on her suggestions."

Maddie was trying valiantly to remember those suggestions the next day as she walked slowly toward the Fine Arts Complex. She was wearing her new black-and-white camp shirt, a black skirt, and her silver earrings. The outfit made her feel confident, and she had put a little gel on her short hair to give it a more interesting look.

"Maddie, I've been following you for a block and I didn't even realize it was you," Mike said, suddenly stepping into stride beside her.

Maddie's heart did its usual flip-flop when she looked at him. "Why's that?" she asked sweetly.

He looked her over. "I don't know. Your hair's different, isn't it? And you don't usually wear black."

"It's all part of the new me," she said fliply.

"I liked the old you," Mike said with a crooked grin.

"You're going to like this one even better," Maddie promised. It was still hard to be flirtatious with Mike, but she thought she was getting the hang of it.

"Where are you headed?" Mike asked.

Maddie hesitated. She didn't want to lie, but she wasn't ready to share her secret with Mike. "I'm going over to the Fine Arts Complex. I . . . left something backstage."

Mike looked at her strangely, and Maddie wondered if he could see right through her story. "I thought you might have had something special going. I mean, you're so dressed up."

"Not really." Maddie laughed nervously. "I just picked up a few new things in Atlanta. You'll be seeing a lot of my new clothes—at least I hope you will."

Mike looked confused by her little attempt at

wit, and Maddie decided to try again. "Maybe I should try out for *Carousel* while I'm over there. It would be fun to play opposite you."

Mike obviously didn't know what to say to that, either. "Uh, sure would," he muttered.

When they got to the Union, Mike stopped. "I have to go to the bookstore. I'll talk to you later." He gave Maddie an awkward little kiss on the cheek and hurried away.

The encounter with Mike didn't exactly boost Maddie's confidence. She had hoped the suggestion of them working together would have excited Mike a little more, even if he did only think it was hypothetical. Fortunately, Maddie didn't have time to ponder the question. Her audition was only five minutes away.

Maddie knew from past experience how these things worked. She'd be asked to wait outside the auditorium until the previous candidate finished. Then she'd go into the almost empty hall, perform for Professor Olin, Ben, and Mrs. Robinson, the musical director. After they thanked her she would leave, making room for the next hopeful. Luckily she wouldn't have to wait long to learn the outcome—Ben had promised he would meet her later in the Union grill to tell her who had been cast.

It was Ben who now came to the door and ushered Maddie backstage. "Break a leg, kid," he whispered.

Maddie closed her eyes and took a few seconds to compose herself. Then she took a deep breath and walked out onstage. With Ben giving her cues from the front row, she read the scene she had picked out from the play. She tried to inject into the role the brashness Erica had suggested. Then it was time to sing the song she had rehearsed. Although it was daunting to sing out into the dark theater, Maddie was pleased when she had finished; she felt she had done a pretty good job. Nevertheless, it was with great relief that she fled out the door into the sunshine, after Professor Olin had thanked her and told her they'd be making their decision that afternoon.

Now that the audition was over, Maddie wanted to erase the experience from her mind, but all the way to the Union, she kept thinking how she had phrased each note and how she had uttered every line of her speech. She was glad when she saw Stacy coming out of the bookstore and begged her to sit down with her at the Union. Maybe a conversation would take her mind off things.

"So, tell me everything," Stacy said once they were seated. "How did it go?"

Maddie made a little face. "All right, I guess. Nobody threw tomatoes."

"Well, that's promising," Stacy laughed.

"I'm going to wait here until Ben comes by to give me the news."

"As a matter of fact, I have some news of my own. I saw Rita today, and she was doing a little informal polling before APA officially votes on our new rushees."

"And?" Maddie asked with interest.

"And it looks like Erica's a shoo-in. Every single girl Rita talked to wanted Erica in."

"What about Liz?"

"Didn't you hear? Liz took herself out of rush. The APA tea was the first and last one she went to."

"That's too bad," Maddie said sincerely. Obviously, her little talk with Liz hadn't done much good. "She really would have been a great addition to any house."

"I agree. I know I can never put myself in Liz's place, but I wish she would have given the girls more of a chance," Stacy said.

"She's probably given people chances—and been let down," Maddie said thoughtfully.

The girls spent the next half hour or so gossiping in between glances at their textbooks. Finally, Stacy stood up and stretched her arms over her head. "I have to get back to the dorm. Will you be all right if I leave you alone here?"

Stacy looked so serious that Maddie had to giggle. "Go ahead, Stace. I'm a big girl. I can handle whatever news I get."

But a few moments after Stacy's departure, she was not so sure. Ben walked through the swinging doors of the Union, and he didn't look happy. Maddie clenched her hands nervously as Ben pulled up a chair.

"You don't have to tell me," she said. "I can tell by the look on your face that I didn't get the part."

Ben patted her hand. "Thanks for making that so easy for me, Maddie. I'm sorry, but the news isn't really all that bad. Professor Olin thought you might do well in the part of Julie Jordan's best friend."

Maddie did know the role: It was a supporting one, with just one song. Although she was happy to know the committee considered her good enough to be in the play, she didn't feel like going through all the trauma of being onstage if she couldn't be Mike's leading lady. "I don't think I'm going to take the role, Ben. It's not sour grapes, but I'd really rather work backstage with you."

Ben actually looked relieved. "Frankly, Maddie, I didn't know what I was going to do without you. But I don't want to take away a chance for you to be out front."

"Don't worry about it. I guess I'm just more suited to behind-the-scenes work. So who are you going to cast as Julie?" Maddie asked as casually as she could.

"Erica Martin."

Maddie felt as though she had just been given a jolt of electricity. "Erica? We spent all last evening together, and she never once mentioned she was thinking of trying out. In fact, she told me all the reasons she didn't want to."

"All I know is she came in a little while after

you, and she was the ultimate Julie Jordan. Sweet, and kind of shy . . ."

"Sweet and shy?" Maddie said incredulously. "That's how she played the part?"

Ben looked puzzled by Maddie's agitated expression. "Sure, that's how the part was written. She was even wearing some cute little flowered blouse with ruffles. Kind of old fashioned . . . hey, there she is." Ben pointed out Erica, who was heading toward their table.

"I've got to talk to you, Maddie," Erica said immediately.

"Yes, you do." Maddie turned to Ben. "Will you please excuse us?"

Ben didn't have to be asked twice. He didn't look as if he wanted to stick around and watch the fireworks.

"So," Maddie began, her arms folded across her chest. "I hear congratulations are in order."

"Maddie, I had *no* idea I'd be picked for the part. And when they did give it to me, I rushed over here because I didn't want you to hear the news from anyone else."

"That was awfully big of you. How did you know I was here?"

"I saw Stacy on my way back to the dorm— that's where I thought you'd be. Listen, I know you're upset, but it was only because of you that I tried out at all."

"Me?"

"Yes, last night you said being in a school production might help me regain my self-confidence. Well, the more I thought about it, the more it seemed like a good idea. So I figured I'd try out. Just going to the audition would be good experience, and I thought I might land a role in the chorus or something . . . nothing big."

"And what about your interpretation?" Maddie said, her anger evident.

"My what?"

"Ben said you played the role sweetly and demurely—the exact opposite of the way you told me to play it."

"I did that on purpose, Maddie. I didn't want to steal your interpretation of the part after we had worked so hard on it. I decided I had to try it a different way."

Maddie sat there for a minute or two without saying anything. Erica certainly had an answer for everything. The problem was, Maddie couldn't tell if she was telling the truth. It certainly looked as though tears were watering behind Erica's eyes—but as Maddie now knew, Erica could be quite an actress.

"Say something Maddie," Erica pleaded. "I really hate the thought of you being upset with me."

Maddie sighed. She supposed she had no proof that Erica had deliberately misled her; her audition certainly could have been a last-minute decision. Still, the thought of Mike and Erica playing those romantic scenes—the very ones she hoped to play—did nothing to cheer her.

Maddie was glad she hadn't accepted an onstage role. She couldn't imagine anything worse than being out in front of an audience trying to act while Mike had his arms around Erica.

"Maddie . . ." Erica began hesitantly.

"It's all right, Erica," Maddie said. She pasted a half-hearted smile on her face. "I guess these things happen sometimes."

Erica jumped up, and her whole demeanor changed. Her eyes, so sad just seconds ago, were sparkling and her smile was as wide as Maddie's was thin. "Thank you, thank you!" she cried. "Do you want to walk home with me?"

"No, I'm going to stay here for a while." Maddie wanted desperately to be left alone to lick her wounds, and she wanted Erica to leave right away: Being around someone so happy was depressing. As she watched Erica make her way out of the Union—after stopping to talk to three or four people—Maddie couldn't help wonder once more if Erica was telling the truth. One thing was for sure, not knowing was going to make living with Erica—and being her sorority sister—very hard, if not impossible.

Chapter 10

Maddie stood at the door of the PizzaRoo, a grimace on her face. It seemed as though she was stepping over Erica wherever she went.

"Who are you frowning at?" Roni asked. "Didn't your mother ever tell you your face could freeze like that?"

"It's Erica, over there in the corner with her friend Kitty."

"I hear she got the role you were after," Roni said sympathetically.

"Yep. She and Mike were entwined in each other's arms last night, practicing their first kiss."

"It's only make-believe," Roni responded gently.

"I hope. Hey, someone's leaving. Let's grab that table."

When the girls got themselves settled, Maddie tried to keep ner mind on the menu, but her eyes kept straying to Erica and Kitty, who were laughing uproariously at something.

"Hey, you're the one who has a date with Mike tonight," Roni said, following her glance.

"That's true." Maddie brightened a little.

"Besides, Erica wouldn't really try to take a boyfriend away from a roommate, would she?"

"I don't know, Roni. She was talking the other night about the bottom line and how important it is."

"As in the business term?"

"Uh-huh. After you add up all the pluses and minuses, what you're left with is the bottom line. Apparently Erica's father thinks that's the most important thing, and I bet Erica does, too."

Roni ran a well-manicured finger around the edge of her menu. "And you think getting Mike is the bottom line for Erica?"

Maddie shrugged. "Could be."

"But, Maddie, why would Erica do all this stuff in such a roundabout way if she's so cutthroat? Wouldn't she just try out for the part of Julie without making up that story? Or go after Mike, for that matter?"

"Maybe she just likes the intrigue."

"Or she may still want to stay on the good side of you and Stacy," Roni said thoughtfully. "After all, if she makes you mad, you could blackball her right out of APA."

"I never thought of that," Maddie said, staring

at Erica and Kitty as they left. For what seemed like the thousandth time she wished she could figure out just what was going on inside Erica's pretty little head.

"But whatever Erica's up to," Roni said, "you can handle it."

"That's your opinion," Maddie answered wryly. Still, Roni's support made her feel better. She was glad she had persuaded Roni to come out with her today. Maddie had broached the subject carefully since everyone had been telling her how depressed Roni was, but when Maddie had suggested pizza for lunch, Roni had agreed immediately. After their order was taken, Maddie launched into the reason she had brought Roni here. "Listen, I know everyone has been on your back lately, but can't you tell me what's bothering you?" she asked.

Roni looked back at her with sad eyes. "I've been trying to figure that out for myself. I guess it all started when I went home at the end of the summer. There's something about me in the same house with my parents; it's like oil and water. Then I came back here, and everything was different. I got depressed."

"Are you still drinking?" Maddie asked cautiously.

"No," Roni said, the relief in her voice palpable. "Not that I haven't wanted to, but for the last week I've stayed away from it."

"That's great," Maddie said, her tone encouraging.

"You know," Roni began slowly, "I never thought of myself as an alcoholic, but I can see what they mean when they talk about one day at a time. When I'm feeling this low it's hard not to take a drink and make myself feel better."

"But, Roni, you seem to have so much insight into your own problems. Doesn't that help?"

Roni laughed. "No. I just know that when I feel bad, I want to drink."

Maddie could see how hard this was for Roni, and she didn't want to prolong the conversation. "Roni, I think you should be proud of how well you're doing. Don't dwell on things you can't change."

"I guess you're right," Roni said listlessly. But Maddie could tell Roni was as depressed as ever, and it worried her that she couldn't help.

Later that night, as she was dressing for her date with Mike, Maddie told Stacy about her lunch with Roni.

"She's really upset about her parents coming down tomorrow. I guess they just drive her up the wall."

Stacy smiled ruefully. "Well, as a daughter whose mother does the same thing, I can sympathize. But unlike my mother, who's usually pretty cold toward me, Roni's parents smother her with affection." Stacy paused. "So, where are you and Mike off to?"

"We're going out for dinner."

"So that's why you're wearing your new

dress." Stacy looked carefully at Maddie. "Are you sure you're not *too* dressed up for Hawthorne Springs?"

"Come on, this isn't that special, is it? What do you think of my hair?" Maddie asked. Once again, she had put some gel on her hair to spike it.

"To tell you the truth, it looks more like a style Roni might wear."

Maddie's face fell. She wished Stacy wasn't quite so honest. "But this is what all the models in the fashion magazines are doing with short hair. It's very trendy."

"You don't always have to be trendy, Maddie," Stacy said gently.

Maddie took a lot of time applying makeup, but she was still ready fifteen minutes early. She wandered around the suite and straightened it up for a while. But when Mike hadn't shown up almost forty-five minutes later, Maddie started to worry. If there was one thing she already knew about Mike, it was that he was dependable.

When the phone rang, Maddie knew it had to be Mike. Sure enough, his deep, distinctive voice came over the wire.

"Maddie?"

"Where are you, Mike?"

"Listen, I'm sorry, but some friends from L.A. were driving to Atlanta and they stopped by on their way. Would it be all right if they joined us for dinner?"

"Of course!" Maddie was delighted that Mike wanted to introduce her to some of his friends.

"Great. We'll be right over."

Maddie spent the next minutes putting on more makeup and adding more gel to her hair. She wanted to look chic enough to meet Mike's L.A. friends. When Mike buzzed the intercom in her room from downstairs, she grabbed her purse and hurried to the reception area where he was waiting for her.

Dressed plainly in a crisp white oxford-cloth shirt and tan pleated chinos, Mike nevertheless looked like an ad in *GQ*. Maddie nervously touched her hair. She hoped she looked okay.

"Where are your friends?" Maddie asked as Mike pushed the front door open for her.

"In the car." He pointed to where a mini van was parked in the driveway. "You're going to love them. Tracy, Jasper, and I go way back."

When Maddie climbed into the back seat of the van she was surprised to see that Tracy and Jasper were old, in their early thirties at least. Initially she was glad she was wearing her new outfit, but then she noticed both Tracy and Jasper were dressed casually.

"Tracy, Jasper, this is my friend Maddie Lerner."

"My friend" didn't sound romantic enough to Maddie, but she tried to hide her disappointment as she greeted them.

"Where are we off to?" Jasper asked Mike as he started the engine.

"Maddie?" Mike turned to her. "Where can we get a decent meal in this town? So far I've only been to places I can walk to," he informed his friends.

Maddie nervously rubbed her thumb against the car seat. She wished she had known she'd be expected to pick a restaurant so she could have talked it over with Stacy. She didn't know what kind of food they wanted, or how much they were willing to spend—and if no one liked it, it would be her fault. "Well, let's see. There's the Harmony House. It's kind of bland, but it's pleasant. Or there's Jake's. It's a really noisy bar but it has good food. There's a steak place in town, but it's a chain restaurant. It's not that great."

"That's it?" Jasper said, rubbing his chin thoughtfully.

"Except for the usual pizza and hamburger places."

"Boy, when you said this town was in the boondocks, Mikey, you weren't kidding," Tracy said with a husky laugh.

Mikey? She calls him Mikey? Maddie thought.

"Let's go to the quietest place," Tracy continued. "We didn't come here just to yell across the table at you."

Maddie proceeded to give Jasper directions to the Harmony and then leaned back in her seat while the conversation went on without her. From what she could gather, Jasper was a teacher at UCLA and Mike had rented a room at their house a few years ago. There was more talk about people Maddie didn't know and places she had never seen and by the time they arrived at the restaurant, Maddie had to blink a few times to keep herself awake.

The Harmony House was a restaurant that prided itself on its plain, down-home fare and its large collection of beer steins that filled the waiting area. There was also a selection of badly painted wildlife pictures lining the walls.

"Oh wow," Jasper said in a stage whisper, "is this place funky, or what?"

Now that they were standing up, Maddie could see that Tracy was a tall, voluptuous woman with raven-black hair that sported just a few strands of gray. Jasper was shorter than she. He wore several gold chains around his neck and a shirt opened almost to the navel, so he could show them off.

"The food's very good here," Maddie said, already feeling as if she had picked the wrong restaurant.

Jasper picked up on her concern. "Hey, no problem, Mad. This place is a trip."

"You're right, Jasper," Tracy chimed in. "We wanted to see the real America as we drove along and this"—she glanced around the room—"is totally *real*."

After they were seated, and had ordered, Jasper said, "So tell me about this play you're in, Mike. *Carousel*, you said? A fine American musical," he added.

Maddie couldn't tell if he was being sarcastic or not.

"Who's your Julie Jordan?" Tracy asked. She lit a cigarette and inhaled deeply.

"A girl named Erica Martin. She's Maddie's roommate."

"Any good?" Jasper asked, taking a cigarette from Tracy's pack.

Mike's eyes lit up, and Maddie's heart fell. "Terrific. She's got a great voice, and a lot of stage presence."

"Hard to imagine that there are any really talented kids in a school this small," Jasper said skeptically.

Maddie thought this remark was insulting, but Mike just laughed along with his friend. "You're right. They only looked at a few other guys for my role, but basically I knew I had it as soon as I showed up. They weren't sure what they were going to do for a female lead. The guy who's running things couldn't find anyone. Apparently, Erica tried out at the last minute."

Maddie's face reddened. Even though Mike had no idea that Maddie had tried out, she knew she had been one of the girls on Ben's "unacceptable" list.

"What about you, Maddie?" Jasper asked as he flicked his ashes into a glass ashtray. "Any theatrical aspirations?"

"I'm strictly behind the scenes," Maddie muttered.

"Did you know Erica was so talented?" Mike asked conversationally.

"No. In fact I've just begun to find out."

"It's not just her voice, although that's great. She has a lot of charisma on stage. It's hard to describe."

Maddie caught Tracy looking at Mike thoughtfully. So she wasn't the only one who thought Mike was talking a little too much about his leading lady. Fortunately, the subject of Erica Martin was dropped during dinner, but what replaced it wasn't much better. Mike, Tracy, and Jasper traded witty anecdotes about the actors and actresses who were friends, or friends of friends, and Maddie had nothing to contribute.

During dessert Maddie launched into a long story about how her father, a true absent-minded professor type, was almost cast in a TV commercial. It had been very funny when it happened, but it certainly lost something in the retelling. And the harder she tried to be witty, the more forced the story became. She ended the anecdote on a limp note with her three dinner companions looking at her a little blankly. Mike rescued her by changing the subject to the regional theater work Tracy and Jasper were going to be doing in Atlanta. Then they moved on to neutral topics such as the weather, the Atlanta Braves, and the best route into the city.

Eliciting a promise that they come to Atlanta to see them, Jasper and Tracy dropped Maddie and Mike off near Rogers House. They walked the few short blocks to the dorm in silence.

Maddie was still smarting over the way the evening had—or had not—gone. She finally decided she had to apologize in order to feel better about it. "Mike," she said softly, "I hope I didn't embarrass you in front of your friends."

"You didn't embarrass me," Mike answered.

"I don't know what happened, I just kept going on and on with that stupid story."

Mike put his arm around Maddie's shoulder. "Hey, don't worry about it. We all get caught in the middle of a dumb story every now and then."

This didn't do much to raise Maddie's spirits. Mike hadn't denied the story was dumb: He had only told her that she shouldn't let its dumbness bother her. "I guess I should be getting in," she said miserably.

"Come on, don't feel bad."

"I don't," Maddie answered, but she was hard pressed to keep the tears glistening in her eyes from falling.

"Look, I hear there's a school dance coming up. What's it called?"

"Fall Ball. It's a tradition to have it when we play Julian College in football."

"Want to go?"

All the worries and insecurities Maddie had felt over the course of the evening dissolved instantly. "I'd love to go, Mike."

"Great. Consider it a date." Then he leaned

down and kissed her on the lips. Maddie would have liked the kiss to last longer, but Mike pulled away, said good night, and left her to wander upstairs.

She took a hot bath to relax, then climbed into bed to mull over the evening. She couldn't figure Mike out. He had asked her to the Fall Ball, so he must like her, but then there was that quick, polite kiss . . . and the look in his eyes when he talked about Erica. After tossing and turning Maddie finally turned over and punched her pillow, determined to stop thinking about it and fall asleep. But she heard the clock on the quad strike twelve and then one. And instead of sleeping, Maddie lay awake, still trying to make sense of Mike.

Chapter 11

It was almost eleven o'clock, and Roni was pacing the living room floor nervously. She wished Sam and Liz would leave the suite before her parents arrived, but neither seemed ready to leave. Sam was sitting on the patio with a stack of books next to her and Liz was reading in her bedroom. At least Angie was gone: What her parents would say about Angie and her hippie garb was more than Roni wanted to imagine.

She looked in the refrigerator vaguely and then slammed it shut. After one more circle around the living room, she walked into the bedroom and shut the door, on the back of which was a full-length mirror. For a second she didn't even recognize herself. Since there was nothing very conservative in her own closet, she had borrowed a dress of Sam's, a pale pink shirtwaist, complete with a little round collar. Her usually wild hair was pulled back into a ponytail, and she was wearing simple pearl earrings, a gift from her parents for her high school graduation. Most of the time Roni got a perverse pleasure out of shocking her parents with her flashy wardrobe, but today she didn't have the heart for the usual battle. She hoped that if she played it their way for once, they could all have a pleasant afternoon and everyone would go away happy. Not very likely, she knew, but a girl could dream.

After taking one final look at herself in the mirror, Roni went into the bathroom and pulled a tube of pale pink lipstick from her makeup bag. She supposed she should also apply some cover-up to the dark circles under her eyes, but before she could, there was a sharp double rap on the front door. It was her mother's knock; she would know it anywhere.

Trying to put a smile on her face, Roni went into the living room and opened the door wide.

"Honey, how *are* you?" Mrs. Davies enveloped Roni in her arms and smothered her against her chest.

Once her mother finally released her, Mr. Davies came over and gave Roni a quick peck on the cheek.

"Take a look around, Mother," Roni said. "Can you believe how nice it is?"

But Mrs. Davies had already begun to examine the new decor. At one time, when she was very young, Mrs. Davies had been a runner-up in a couple of beauty contests. Now she was more matronly, but under the excess weight and the abundantly applied makeup was a glimmer of that pretty girl. The turned-up nose was Roni's, and so was the fading auburn hair. "Very nice," she said, touching the soft teal fabric on the couch. "Don't you think so, Walter?"

Mr. Davies gave a noncommittal grunt.

"Yes, this is much more suitable for my little Daphne Veronica than that awful room she had last year."

Roni cringed. She tried very hard to forget that her first name was Daphne, but with her mother around to remind her she didn't have much luck.

"Hello, Mrs. Davies, Mr. Davies," Sam said, coming in from the patio. "How nice to see you again."

"Samantha, dear. You're looking well."

"Thank you." Sam responded politely.

"Samantha's such a nice girl, isn't she?" Mrs. Davies directed the question to her husband as though Sam weren't right in front of her. It was a bad habit of hers, this talking through and around people as if they weren't there, and it drove Roni crazy.

"She certainly is," Mr. Davies agreed.

"Sit down, Samantha." Mrs. Davies waved Sam to a chair as though she was the hostess.

"Now," Mrs. Davies continued, "tell me about

this Mrs. Wentworth who donated the money for the renovation. Is she one of the Alabama Wentworths?"

Out of the corner of her eye, Roni could see Sam trying to keep a straight face. "I really don't know, Mrs. Davies."

"Well, I suppose it doesn't matter, but I do know some Wentworths in Mobile, and I could find out." She settled herself heavily in the armchair and directed her attention to Roni's attire. "I must say, dear, that's a prettier dress than those awful tiger striped things you usually wear."

"Thank you, Mother," Roni said. She exchanged a faint smile with Sam.

"But it doesn't look like very good quality material. Really, the whole thing seems rather cheaply made. Where in the world did you get it?"

Roni blushed bright red. "I picked it up . . . somewhere."

"One can always tell cheaply made clothes, darling. I thought you knew that. We give you a generous clothing allowance, but if you need more, let us know, okay, honey?"

Roni stood and stared at her mother. She folded her arms across her chest. There was an awful silence.

Finally, Sam jumped up. "Would anyone like some lemonade?"

"How lovely. Well, yes, I would," replied Mrs. Davies.

"I'll have some, too, Samantha," Mr. Davies answered. "Nice of you to ask." He looked pointedly at Roni, who refused to meet his gaze.

"Oh, it's no trouble," Sam said. It was obvious to Roni that Sam was glad to have an excuse to leave the tense atmosphere, even if she was only moving a few feet away.

"Now where are these other roommates of yours?" Mrs. Davies asked with a frown.

"Angie is out, and I think Liz is in her bedroom studying." Roni answered shortly.

Mrs. Davies accepted the glass Sam handed her with a nod of thanks. "What do *you* think of these girls, Samantha?"

"I think they're very nice. And Roni and I are both enjoying acting as their big sisters."

Sam was trying to put a positive face on things, but Roni knew this subject was the wrong thing to bring up.

"I don't know how it is in Illinois," Mrs. Davies said indignantly, "but here, we do not act as sisters to those who are not our own."

Roni nervously rubbed her hands together. Sam hadn't dated Aaron Goldberg, social activist, all those months for nothing. As diplomatic as she was, Sam had her breaking point—and Roni could see that it was very close. "Say," Roni said loudly, "it's getting to be lunchtime and I'm starved. You promised me a decent meal, remember?"

"Yes, of course," Mrs. Davies replied, temporarily distracted by the subject of food.

"Though I did think perhaps we should eat in the cafeteria, just to see what they're feeding y'all."

Roni let out a deep sigh. "There's no point, Mother. You can't change the food, and all eating in the cafeteria would do is deprive me of a decent meal."

"Daphne's right, Mother." Mr. Davies stood up and stretched. "Let's go to that little country inn just outside of Bensenville."

"Well, if that's what you would like, Walter," Mrs. Davies deferred.

"It is. That was the plan, and we'll stick to the plan." He had been saying that for as long as Roni could remember. Obviously, it was the army colonel in him.

"What about you, Samantha?" Mrs. Davies asked. "Surely you'd like a change of pace from your usual dining room fare."

"Thank you, but I have a previous engagement," Sam said stiffly.

Mrs. Davies frowned. "Are you still dating that young man from New York?"

"No," Sam said quietly. "We broke up."

Roni could feel her temperature rising. She appreciated Sam's restraint, but why did her mother have to say things like that? It was nobody's business whom Sam dated; certainly it was not the concern of Mary Louise Davies.

"Let's go," Roni said, picking up her purse. She had promised herself that she wouldn't let her mother get to her today, but if they didn't leave immediately, Roni knew she was going to blow her stack. She could see a very long afternoon ahead.

On the ride out to Bensenville, Roni sat in the backseat of the huge Cadillac. She opened the window so the breeze against her ear blocked out her mother's voice, but once they were seated in the charming little country inn her father had picked out, there was no avoiding Mrs. Davies's constant harangue. It was all couched in the nicest of terms, with plenty of *honey*'s and *sugar*'s thrown in, but as usual it came down to the same old things: Why didn't Roni get better grades? Why couldn't she have joined a sorority? Didn't she want to transfer to a more prestigious school when she was a junior? Had she really stopped wearing all those ridiculous clothes? It was all Roni could do to eat some of her pasta salad, all the while repeating over and over to herself, "She's not going to get to me."

As the coffee was served, Roni glanced over at her father. He never hassled her in the same way her mother did, but the emotion she most often felt from him was disdain. Had she ever measured up to his exact standards? She didn't think so. She stirred her coffee silently. Mrs. Davies's smothering intensity never felt like love, and neither did her father's wintery smiles.

On the ride home, Roni was relieved to hear that her parents would be leaving shortly. "You know, when I talked to you, I totally forgot that

tonight is the country club dance," Mrs. Davies
said. "You could drive back with us and attend.
I'm sure it would be lovely. They always have a
nice group of young people."

"Sorry, I can't make it," Roni answered right
away. She was sure it would be anything but
lovely, with a lot of prissy girls and snobby boys
in attendance.

"Do you have a date, Hon?"

"No, but I have a lot of studying to do." That,
she thought, ought to make her mother happy.
But when she looked up, she saw a frown on her
mother's face.

"Studying on a Saturday night? You really
should plan your time a little more carefully.
You should have a date lined up."

Roni could have reminded her mother that
just moments ago she had pronounced none of
the boys on the Hawthorne campus suitable for
her daughter, but what was the point? Her
mother was always right, and nothing she could
say would change that.

Roni hoped that since her parents had to go
back to Atlanta, they would just drop her off at
the dorm, but when they pulled up in front of
Rogers House, her father pulled into a parking
space. "We have another half hour or so, let's
just go up and visit," Mrs. Davies said.

Isn't that what we have been doing? Roni
wondered.

Roni hoped that none of her roommates was
in the suite, but when she arrived, Liz was

watching television in the living room. Reluctantly, she made the introductions.

"Could you switch off the television, Liz? I'd like to talk to you a little bit," Mrs. Davies asked—or, rather, commanded.

"Would anyone like some lemonade?" Roni asked, trying to forestall her mother's inevitable inquisition. She wished she could just take Liz by the shoulders and tell her to get out of the room. Roni felt like a bystander watching an impending car accident, but unable to stop it.

"I understand you're here on scholarship," Mrs. Davies said, ignoring Roni's offer. She placed her purse on the coffee table and sat down on the couch.

"That's right," Liz said. She looked a little puzzled by the direction the conversation was taking.

"And you were at Bloomfield on scholarship as well?"

"That's right."

"I must ask you something, my dear. Doesn't it bother you to keep attending schools where there are so few of your kind?"

"My '*kind*'?" Liz said, obviously not pleased with Mrs. Davies' choice of words.

"Mother . . ." Roni started to say, but her mother just plowed on.

"Now I hope you won't be offended, but I'm a plain-speaking woman, aren't I, Walter?" Mr. Davies nodded in confirmation. "For your own sake, don't you feel uncomfortable where you're a minority?"

Liz laughed. "Mrs. Davies, I'm a minority everywhere I go."

Mrs. Davies was a little flustered, but she didn't give up. "Yes of course, but it must be very difficult for you here. For instance, how will you ever find someone to date here at Hawthorne?"

"You're the second person who has asked me that. It seems like you all are afraid I'm going to start dating the white boys or something," Liz commented.

Mrs. Davies let out a small gasp. "Have you absolutely *no* manners?"

"Someone in this room doesn't," Liz said, standing up. "And I don't have to listen to this."

"Liz, I'm sorry!" Roni cried, as Liz slammed the door to her room firmly behind her.

"Whatever are you apologizing to her for?" Mrs. Davies asked.

Roni whirled around, all the pent-up fury of the day spilling out of her. "Because, Mother, you were rude to her. Rude!"

"Now, dear, you know that class has its privileges."

"Class?" Roni yelled. "You don't have any class. Your mother may have been in the social register, and your father's family may go back to the glory of the Old South, but you, Mother, have no idea what common courtesy even means!"

"Daphne Veronica!" her mother gasped.

Mr. Davies's face turned beet-red. "You're my daughter, now hold your tongue."

"Go ahead, stick up for her. Can't you see how she embarrasses me with her phony morals and genteel manners that just hurt the people I care about?"

Roni ran out of the suite. She didn't bother to close the door behind her. She could hear her father's voice calling her name down the hall, but she didn't stop. Feeling around in her pocket for her car keys, she was glad when she found them nestled under a Kleenex. She didn't have her license, but she didn't care about that. As long as she had her keys, she could make her escape.

Roaring out of the parking lot, Roni drove around aimlessly for a while. It was difficult to keep her mind on the road. Her parents had been embarrassing her all her life, but this was the last straw. She didn't know why she even bothered to try to please them. From now on she was going to have fun—the heck with manners and morals. Roni Davies wasn't going to wind up some society matron. She was going to live for the moment, starting right now.

Eventually Roni ended up at the edge of Greek town. She decided to park and walk around for a while, just to see if anything was happening. She hadn't gone much more than a block when she ran into Phil Morantz, a guy she had dated once or twice last year.

"Hey, Roni, what happened to you?" Phil wanted to know, looking her up and down.

"What do you mean?"

"Well, that's a pretty weird outfit for Roni Davies."

She looked down at Sam's wrinkled pink dress. "You're right." She laughed. "It's not my style. I was trying out a new image, but it didn't work."

"Hey, you don't need a new image. Certainly not that one. You're too much of a party girl to be pretty in pink."

"Well, guess what? This party girl is looking for a party. Know of one?"

"I sure do. The Delts are having a barbeque, and I was just heading over there. Want to come?"

"Sure, but tell you what. I'll meet you over there in about a half hour."

"Okay, sounds good. See you later."

Roni hurried back to the car and drove over to Whiz!, her favorite store. She quickly picked out a wild print dress with a plunging neckline and then she borrowed a comb from the sales-girl. She wasn't about to risk going back to the suite. Her parents had probably left, but Roni couldn't face Liz. Besides, Roni didn't want to think about her family, or Liz, or what had happened. Tonight she was going to party.

The Delts had provided several kegs of beer for their barbeque guests, and Roni tried her best to make a dent in all of them. By the time the stars were twinkling in the evening sky, Roni was as bombed as she had ever been in her life. She was vaguely aware that in the midst of all her wild dancing and drinking Phil had come up to her several times and told her to take it easy, but had just ignored him. Now that she wasn't feeling very well, she looked around for him with bleary eyes, hoping to ask him to take her home.

Roni staggered into the Delt house, ignoring the people who seemed to be pointing at her. Trying as hard as she could to walk in a straight line, she stumbled on a rip in the carpet and practically fell flat on her face. Finally she saw Phil in the corner talking to a girl she didn't know. Mustering whatever strength she had left, she went over to him. "Phil, I'd like to go home now."

Phil looked at her and raised one eyebrow. "I'm talking to someone, Roni."

The girl gave Roni a pitying glance. "Oh, take her home, Phil. She'll never make it there by herself."

Roni cringed with embarrassment while Phil thought about it. "Will you wait for me?" he asked the girl. When she nodded, he grabbed Roni's arm and led her to the door. "I'll be right back," he called over his shoulder.

As soon as Roni was safely perched in the passenger's seat of her car, she started to cry.

"I'll drive you home," Phil said coldly, "but quit crying. And from now on, if you can't hold your liquor, stay home."

Roni put her hand over her mouth to muffle her sobs, but the tears still fell down her cheeks.

When Phil pulled up in front of the dorm a few minutes later he told Roni he was going to drive her car back to the party. "I don't want to waste any more time, and you won't need it in your condition, anyway. I'll bring it back tomorrow," he said.

Roni nodded, then she dragged herself out of the car and walked unsteadily into the dorm. She was lucky enough to find the suite. She kicked off her shoes and collapsed on her bed fully clothed.

Roni had no idea what time it was when she awoke. It was dark out, and Sam was snoring lightly in the next bed. On tiptoes, Roni went to the bathroom and located the aspirin: She needed something to quell her raging headache fast. She looked in the mirror briefly. Between crying and sleeping, her makeup had streaked all over her face. Roni grabbed a cotton ball and removed it with some lotion, then splashed her face with cold water. Tiptoeing into the bedroom, she changed into a nightgown and lay back down on her bed. But sleep wouldn't come—too many ugly images flashed in front of her eyes. Finally, she decided to get up and try the living room couch.

Roni was startled by the sight of a figure on the balcony, then she saw that it was only Liz. Roni turned to go hide in the bedroom, but she knew she would have to apologize to Liz sooner or later.

She whispered Liz's name, and the girl peered into the living room. "Roni?"

Roni moved out onto the balcony. A warm breeze was blowing through the trees, and the air seemed soft and peaceful.

"Nice, huh?" Liz said, not looking at her.

Roni nodded.

"The earth's a fine place—when all the people are asleep."

"Listen, Liz," Roni began uncomfortably, "I want to apologize for my parents."

"Hey, you can't be responsible for what they say and do."

"I know I haven't been very friendly this semester, but it wasn't because of . . . of you."

Liz chuckled, "I know. You've been rude to everybody."

Roni smiled a tiny smile. "Well, just so you know I'm not discriminating."

"What happened to you tonight?" Liz asked, turning serious.

Roni's immediate thought was to lie and pretend nothing had happened, but she realized that Liz knew what kind of condition she had come home in. After all, Roni had certainly been sprawled out on her bed for everyone to see. Roni moved to one of the patio chairs and sat down, facing away from Liz. "You met my parents today. Is it any wonder I feel like escaping once in a while by drinking?"

Liz sat across the table, so Roni had to face

her. "I guess not. But when you drink, who are you escaping?"

Roni examined her nails. "They drive me crazy," she went on, looking up into Liz's eyes. "It's been mixed messages all my life. I was their sweet, wonderful little girl, but then nothing I did was ever good enough for them. Finally, I couldn't stand it anymore. I just had to be my own person."

"So the person who wears wild clothes and drinks a lot is the real Roni Davies?"

"Maybe it is," a defiant Roni answered.

"You forget, Roni, I remember you from way back."

"You didn't really know me," Roni countered.

"No, but I saw you around, and I heard the other girls talking about you. You were considered one of the nicest and smartest girls at Bloomfield. I also remember the time there were some thefts and a bunch of kids decided that Judy, one of the scholarship students, must have been the guilty party. But you didn't believe it, and you nosed around until you found some evidence that proved it was one of the delivery men who came in and out of the building."

"You remember that?" Roni asked.

"Of course. I thought you were a regular Nancy Drew. To say nothing of the fact that you went out of your way to help a girl you hardly knew."

"I knew Judy wasn't the type to steal," Roni muttered.

"And you proved that. So now you're trying to tell me that you've changed, you don't care about other people now, you're suddenly dumb, so you get bad grades, and the most important thing in your life is partying and drinking."

Roni's face crumbled and she put her head in her hands. "No."

"No, of course not," Liz said quietly.

"But do my parents have to be so overbearing and disapproving all the time? When I'm around them, all I want to do is something wild so they'll notice me."

"They'll certainly notice you if you wind up dead someday," Liz said matter-of-factly.

"What?" Roni jerked her head up.

"You heard me. If you crack up the car or get into some other kind of trouble when you're drunk, they'll notice you, but so what? Who are you hurting? Your parents may not be the way you'd like, but you can't change them. The only person whose behavior you can control is your own."

Roni bit at a fingernail. "So you think I'm just rebelling against my parents? Without a cause?"

Liz's brown eyes were serious, but gentle. "I'm not an expert in psychology Roni, but, I do know this much: The way you feel about your folks is causing you to do things you don't like. Maybe there are other reasons for your behavior, too. Either way, it wouldn't hurt to talk to somebody about this. They have counselors at the Student Life building, you know."

"I know. I even talked to someone last year when I cracked up Stacy's car. But then I was sure my behavior was just a passing phase, and had to do with drinking and freshman year."

"And now?"

Roni thought for a minute. "Now I see my problems go a lot deeper than just using alcohol for a good time."

"Well, now you have another piece of the puzzle," Liz approved.

Roni didn't say a word for a long while. Finally, she lifted her head and said, "Thank you."

"Hey, I didn't do anything." Liz smiled.

"I think you did," Roni replied, smiling back at her.

In the eastern sky, the tiniest sliver of light was cutting through the darkness. "I haven't even asked you what you're doing out here this time of night," Roni said.

Liz's eyes were dark and luminous. "I couldn't sleep. I had some thinking to do."

"Do you want to talk about it? I'd sure like to return the favor."

"I guess I was wondering about something your mother said. Maybe I'm *not* in the right place."

"You're not going to listen to anything she came up with, are you?" Roni cried.

"Hey, there was nothing she said that I hadn't thought about already. Hawthorne might not be the best college for me."

"I don't think you've given it a chance," Roni argued.

"You could be right," Liz agreed, "but I sure haven't felt very comfortable here."

Roni spoke hesitantly. "Are you sure you're not partially to blame for that?"

"I don't know. I'm the first person in my family to go to college, Roni. I'm not sure what to expect—what's normal and what's not. I just want to do the best I can—for me and for my parents."

"You've only been here a little while, Liz. You'll work things out."

"Maybe. But I've got a lot of thinking to do."

"We both do," Roni said, looking up at the fading stars. "We both do!"

Chapter 12

"Erica, please raise your arms a little."

Erica finally focused in on Linda, the costumer, who was hemming her sprigged cotton frock. "Sorry," she said curtly. Erica was too busy thinking to pay attention. She hated it when things didn't go her way, and right now that's just what was happening. It wasn't the dress—it was Mike. Oh, being in Mike's arms every evening during rehearsals was wonderful, but he still didn't seem to be thinking of her as a real-life romance. Still, there was something in the way he kissed her and the way he lightly touched her hair when the kiss was finished that made Erica believe he wasn't just acting.

As she turned to allow Linda better access to the dress, Erica noticed Jimmy Black walking by.

Mike was fairly even tempered, but for some reason he and Jimmy, the head of the scenery crew, didn't get along at all. They had butted heads almost from the day rehearsal had started, and once they had a shouting match that could be heard up and down the hall. A plan began to develop in Erica's mind: Maybe there was a way to use Jimmy and Mike's hostility to her own advantage.

Later that afternoon, Erica spotted Jimmy alone in a corner, hammering the poles of the carousel together. She sidled up to him. When he looked up from his work, Erica gave him a special smile. "How's it going, Jimmy?"

He wiped his sweaty forehead with the back of his hand. "Hot."

"The scenery looks great," she enthused. "I can't wait to see the carousel go up."

Jimmy smiled. "We found some antique carousel horses in a shop in Atlanta, and the owners are going to lend them to us for the run of the show. That'll be a nice touch."

"This is going to be a great show," Erica assured him, "but I'm getting so nervous about my part."

"You? Nervous?" Jimmy scoffed. "You don't have a nervous bone in your body."

"I do, too," Erica pouted.

"Maybe we could go out sometime soon and I could do something to boost your morale."

Jimmy's tone was casual, but what he said made Erica think her plan would definitely work.

Erica twirled a strand of her dark hair. "That would be nice. We could go to that party Ben's having. It sounds like fun," Erica prompted.

"Well, sure. I was thinking of a date by ourselves, but that would be okay."

"Okay. Let me know what time," Erica said. Before Jimmy could say anything else, Erica had disappeared down the hall, looking for Mike.

It was never very difficult to find him; there were usually a couple of admiring females around to point the way. But luckily for Erica, this afternoon Mike was alone in the men's dressing room, going over the script. She peeked in the door and watched him silently for a moment. He was sprawled out on the worn leather couch, and his long legs dangled over one of the arms. As he read, a shock of his dark hair fell into his eyes. With an impatient motion, Mike brushed his hair back, and just this small, intimate gesture was enough to make Erica's heart beat a little faster. She had gone out with many boys in her time, but no one like Mike. She had to have him. She just had to!

Clearing her throat, she tapped lightly at the door. "Mike, can I talk to you for a minute?"

Mike looked up from the script with an expression of annoyance, which faded when he saw who was in the doorway. "Sure, Erica," he said. "Come on in."

"I don't want to bother you, but the truth is,

Mike, I've got a problem, and I just don't know who else to turn to."

Mike motioned to the scratched wooden chair next to the couch and sat upright. "Is this about the play?"

Erica sat down, her knees almost touching Mike's. "No, it's personal."

Mike looked a little uncomfortable. "I'm not very good with personal problems, Erica."

"I don't know what it is," she almost whispered, "but I just feel like I can confide in you."

Mike cleared his throat. "Well, you can give it a try."

"Thanks." She gave him her most dazzling smile. "Well," she began, "you know Jimmy Black, don't you?"

Mike's face hardened. "I sure do. That guy's been giving me a hard time ever since I got to campus. He seems to have some sort of grudge against guys from L.A., especially if they've been in show business."

"Gee, I didn't know you two didn't get along," Erica exclaimed innocently.

"That's an understatement," Mike said curtly. "So what's this all about?"

"Jimmy's been wanting me to go out with him for a while, but I've always said no. I just didn't feel comfortable with him for some reason."

"Because he's a jerk," Mike said, tossing his script over to the side of the couch. Erica could see he was getting more interested in her plight.

"Yes, but now he asked me to the cast party we're having on Friday night, and I said I'd go."

Mike frowned. "Why did you do that?"

"I just couldn't think of a reason for putting him off anymore," Erica replied, looking miserable.

"So now you have to spend the evening with him."

"Yes, and I'm sure I can handle him, but . . ."

"You mean you think he might try something?" Mike asked, surprised.

Erica stood up. "I'm sorry. This is ridiculous. It's just that I feel I can depend on you, like a big brother or something, and I thought . . . oh, never mind."

Mike put a restraining hand on Erica's arm. She sank slowly back into her chair. "Hey, don't worry about it. You just want me to keep an eye on you, is that it?"

Erica nodded mutely.

"Maybe you should just tell Jimmy to get lost."

"I don't want to do that. It would make for hard feelings and that wouldn't be good for the show."

"All right." Mike smiled. "Since you're being so noble, the least I can do is play guardian angel."

"Oh, thank you," Erica gushed. Knowing her mission was accomplished, she told Mike she wouldn't take up any more of his time and left the dressing room. She almost bumped into

Maddie, headed in Mike's direction. "Mike's a little busy, right now, Maddie," Erica informed her.

"I don't think he's too busy to see me," Maddie said.

"He's working on the scene where he gets stabbed, so he needs to concentrate."

"I guess I shouldn't disturb him, then," Maddie wavered.

"Whatever. Just thought I'd warn you." When she turned the corner, Erica poked her head around to see what Maddie would do. She was pleased to see her roommate walking dejectedly off toward Ben's office. *It's a good thing that Maddie is so gullible*, Erica thought happily. *It makes things a lot easier.*

The night of Ben's party, the weather turned hot and sultry once again. For a change, Erica had the suite to herself and used the opportunity to take a leisurely bubble bath; afterwards, she sprinkled herself liberally with heavily perfumed talcum powder. She wondered what in the world she should wear as she rifled through her closet. Although her fashion-conscious mother had always insisted that women never wear white after Labor Day, the warm weather in Georgia certainly made her ivory off-the-shoulder dress an obvious choice.

The dress was certainly a hit with Jimmy when he came to pick her up. His wolf whistle could be heard up and down the corridor. Jimmy tried to make conversation with Erica as they drove over to Ben's, but Erica was lost in a world of future possibilities. There was only one boy she was thinking of tonight, and it wasn't Jimmy.

By the time they arrived at Ben's together, the party was in full swing. Ben's apartment was small, but he had obviously gone all out for this get-together. He was dashing around the apartment, getting people drinks, setting out dips, and even taking canapes from the tiny oven in his cluttered kitchen.

"I didn't know you cooked, Ben," Erica commented as she tasted one of the mushroom hors d'oeuvres Ben offered her.

"I don't cook," he corrected. "I warm things up."

"Well, they're good, anyway," Erica said, daintily swallowing a bite. She took another one and fed it to Jimmy, who was delighted by the sudden attention.

"Pretty good stuff," he agreed.

"So are you," Erica said flirtatiously.

By some sixth sense, Erica knew the moment Maddie and Mike walked into the apartment. She glanced in Mike's direction, and he gave her an inquiring look, as if to ask if everything with Jimmy was cool. Erica nodded and made a discreet "okay" sign with her thumb and forefinger.

The room was filled with good-natured banter that could barely be heard over the music Ben was playing on the stereo. While most of the other guests, including Maddie and Mike, were sitting around talking, Erica and Jimmy spent a good part of the evening dancing. As the evening wore on, Jimmy's arms grew increasingly tight around Erica's waist. Erica could see that Mike was noticing all this out of the corner of his eye. And every time Mike looked in her direction, Erica put on a distressed expression, as though Jimmy's embrace was something she'd like to wiggle out of as soon as possible.

But when Mike went into the kitchen to help Ben refill people's glasses, Erica whispered in Jimmy's ear, "Why don't we go out on the back porch for a while? It's not so crowded out there—if you know what I mean."

Jimmy's homely face brightened. "Sure," he said, maneuvering her toward the kitchen before she could change her mind. As they walked out the back door, Erica made sure Mike noticed them. She prided herself on dramatic exits, and this was one of her best yet.

"Whew," Erica said, fanning herself with her hand. "It was certainly getting hot in there."

"It sure was," Jimmy agreed. He put his hands gently on her bare shoulders. "Of course, I wouldn't mind if it got a little hot out here."

Erica didn't protest as Jimmy pulled her toward him. Maybe she'd have to give up one kiss, but that wouldn't be so bad if she played her cards right. Jimmy was just pressing his lips against hers when she heard the unmistakable squeak of the screen door. Opening one eye, she saw Mike standing in the doorway. With a twisting motion, she wrenched herself out of

Jimmy's arms. "Leave me alone!" she cried loudly.

"What do you mean?" Jimmy exclaimed. He placed his hands firmly on Erica's shoulders.

"You heard her," Mike said, striding up to them. "She wants you to take your crummy hands off of her."

Jimmy turned toward Mike, his hand already curled into a fist. "Hey, who asked you, movie star."

Mike grabbed Erica's hand and pulled her away from Jimmy. "Just say good night, pal. Erica's made her feelings pretty clear."

"We were doing just fine until you showed up, Genovese," Jimmy said—right before he took a swing at Mike.

Ben came storming out of the house just in time to shove Jimmy's arm before it connected with Mike's face. "Hey, nobody hits my leading man!" he yelled.

Erica gave a little scream, and the porch seemed to fill instantly with guests. Maddie pushed her way to the front of the group. "What's going on here?" she asked.

"Jimmy started something with Erica that she didn't want him to finish," Mike said, his voice shaking.

"That's not true," Jimmy protested. "Tell them, Erica."

But Erica, tears streaming down her face only said, "I'm really sorry about all this, everyone. I want to go home."

"I'll take you," Mike and Jimmy said in unison. Maddie looked at Mike with a hurt expression in her eyes.

"No, I don't want anyone to take me home," Erica insisted. "I'll go by myself."

"No way," Ben said firmly. "*I'll* drive you home, if you want to go. The rest of you guys stay and enjoy the party." Then he cast a doubtful glance at Mike and Jimmy. "Can I trust you two guys to act civilized while I'm gone?"

"Don't worry about that," Jimmy answered, rubbing his arm where Ben had grabbed him. "I'm out of here. And you better watch this one, Ben," he said bitterly, gesturing toward Erica. "She might try something on the way home."

The instant Erica was gone, everyone started talking about what had happened. But Mike just kept shaking his head and didn't say a word.

"What did happen?" Maddie asked, as soon as she could pull Mike away from the crowd.

"You, too?" he snapped.

Maddie fell silent. It didn't seem unreasonable to wonder why her date had almost gotten slugged over another girl, but apparently she wasn't going to hear the story from him. "Do you want to leave?" she asked quietly.

"Yes. Do you mind?"

"Of course not. I'll get my things."

It was a long and silent walk home, and as much as Maddie was bursting with questions, she was afraid voicing them would only provoke another outburst.

When they reached the outskirts of campus, Mike finally turned to her. "I'm sorry about all this, Maddie. Jimmy just rubs me the wrong way. He has from day one."

"Was he really hurting Erica?" Maddie asked tentatively.

Mike's voice took on a sharp edge. "She never really wanted to go out with him. She knew he was only after one thing."

Maddie wondered silently how Mike knew how Erica felt, but she didn't dare ask.

They came to one of the stone benches that dotted the campus, and Mike gestured for Maddie to sit down on it. "Look, Maddie, I know this was a lousy evening for you, but I couldn't just let Jimmy take advantage of Erica. The guy's a creep."

"I'm sure you did what you thought you had to," Maddie said carefully.

"That's right, I did," Mike said, running his hands through his hair. "I just hope Ben and the others don't think I'm too much of a hothead."

Maddie reached over, removed Mike's hand from his forehead, and held it in her own. "You were just trying to help, Mike. That's the kind of person you are. You wouldn't ignore someone if you thought he or she was in trouble."

Mike looked at Maddie with grateful eyes. "You do understand."

"Of course I do," Maddie said soothingly. Despite her inner turmoil, Maddie was trying very hard to be as calm and attentive as she could.

Suddenly Mike got to his feet. "Let's get back to Rogers. I want to see if Erica's all right."

Maddie's heart sank. Mike's protective feelings—if that's what they were—were still operating in full force. But they were for Erica, not her. Maddie felt let down, but she simply nodded and tried to keep up with Mike as he hurried toward Rogers House.

When they entered the suite, the living room was dark. Maddie turned on the light and tiptoed over to Erica's bedroom.

"She's asleep," she said quietly. "I don't think we should wake her."

Mike shook his head. "No, as long as she's all right, that's all I wanted to know."

"Don't worry, she's fine." Maddie said in a slightly sarcastic voice. Mike didn't even notice.

"I guess I should be going," Mike said, stifling a small yawn. "It's been a long day. And an even longer night."

It didn't sound as if Mike had enjoyed their date at all, Maddie thought, distressed that she'd been such a poor date—even if she had been upstaged.

"Maybe tomorrow night will be better," Maddie suggested wanly.

Mike stared blankly at Maddie.

"The Fall Ball?" Maddie hoped he hadn't forgotten completely.

Mike's face cleared. "Oh, sure. I just wasn't thinking there for a second. Sorry. What time do you want me to pick you up?"

Maddie put the most coquettish smile she could muster on her face. "As early as possible," she said softly.

"Well, maybe around seven, then?" Mike said uncomfortably.

Maddie batted her eyes at him. "That would be great." She reached up, put her arms around his neck and gave him a kiss. It was totally out of character for her, but she figured it was a very L.A. thing to do. When Mike started to respond, Maddie was satisfied that she was making all the right moves.

Finally he broke away. "Look, it's geting late, and we don't want to wake Erica."

No, we certainly wouldn't want to wake poor little Erica, Maddie thought spitefully.

After Mike was gone, Maddie went to her empty bedroom and threw herself facedown on the bed. It killed her to see Mike's concern over Erica and yet . . . there was that passionate kiss. She still couldn't figure out Mike. Maybe he was waiting for her to make more moves, like she had tonight. Maybe he wanted their relationship to go further—that could explain why he was so hot and so cold toward her. Maddie rolled over and stared at the ceiling. Mike was no babe in the woods and if she wanted to keep him, she just might have to show him she wasn't, either. The thought scared her, but so did the idea of losing Mike.

Chapter 13

Maddie woke up the next morning determined to confront Erica and see if she could get to the bottom of the previous night's incident. But as soon as she realized the sun was streaming in through the window, Maddie's heart sank. It was late, probably close to ten o'clock, and there was a very good chance that Erica was gone. Sure enough, a quick trip to the other bedroom revealed two empty beds. The only sign of Erica was a white linen envelope lying on Erica's dresser. Maddie turned it over and saw the Alpha Pi Alpha crest emblazoned on it: Erica had received her bid to become an APA pledge.

Maddie sat down on Jean's bed, the torn envelope still in her hand. This shouldn't surprise her. After all, it was just a few days ago that she, along with the rest of the Alpha Pi, had voted on their prospective sorority sisters. There had been some discussion on each of the girls, but no one had received a more enthusiastic welcome than Erica. "Adorable," "sweet," and "really cool" were just a few of the adjectives mentioned, and the vote had been unanimously favorable.

Maddie began tearing the envelope's corner into small bits. She wasn't sure she could have blackballed Erica—even now she only had a few suspicions about her character—but the thought of being in a sisterhood with her wasn't a happy one. One rite of the APA initiation involved the sisters swearing lifelong friendship and fidelity to one another. A mirthless chuckle escaped Maddie's lips. Being friends with Erica forever was something she couldn't quite imagine. And as for fidelity, it didn't seem to be one of Erica's strong suits.

Maddie glanced over at the Mickey Mouse clock Jean had brought with her from Idaho. It was later than she thought, almost noon. If she wanted to make lunch in the Commons, she'd better get dressed and ready to go.

After a long shower, Maddie felt a lot better. She had done some pretty heavy thinking while the hot water massaged her skin, and she had decided the best thing to do was stick to her plan of last night—have a frank talk with Erica whenever she could find her again, and hold on to Mike at all costs.

Maddie had just finished dressing when she heard a knock at the front door. Grabbing a comb and running it through her wet hair, she opened the door to Pam, who looked worried.

"Maddie, I'm so glad you're here."

"Why? What's wrong?"

"Your phone's off the hook, so the operator gave the message to me."

"What message?" Maddie asked, her heart beating a little more rapidly.

"It was from a neighbor of your Aunt Fitty. She said your aunt wasn't feeling well and that she was going to take her to the hospital. She asked that you meet them there."

Maddie's hand flew to her neck. "Is it serious?"

Pam put her arm around Maddie's shoulder and led her over to the couch. "She didn't say. She . . . mentioned it might be your aunt's heart."

"What was the woman's name?"

"Jeannie Smith."

"That doesn't sound familiar, but I don't know all my aunt's friends. What hospital was she going to?"

"The local hospital is what she said. Is there more than one?"

"I . . . I don't think so." Maddie racked her brain trying to remember exactly where the hospital was located. "There's one called Western Springs. And there's another, too, come to think of it, a small Catholic one. St. Joseph's."

"How are you going to get over there?" Pam asked. "I've got a doctor's appointment, but I could cancel it and drive you."

"No, don't do that," Maddie protested. "Maybe I could get ahold of Stacy or Roni."

"I just saw Roni walking down the hall," Pam said. "Let me go explain the situation to her and see if she can drive you out there."

When Pam left the room, all sorts of horrible thoughts began flying around Maddie's mind. Fitty was always so sweet to her and so generous, and Maddie hadn't even called her since she arrived at school. That was the worst part— if something happened to Fitty, she'd feel just awful.

Then another terrible thought struck her. Fall Ball! What if she didn't make it back in time? Hurrying over to the phone, she dialed Mike's number with shaky fingers. He was out, so Maddie left a confused message with his roommate. "Just tell him my aunt was taken sick and I'll try to be back by seven or so."

"And if you're not?" the boy on the other end asked.

"Tell him I'll call."

By the time Maddie finished her call and checked her wallet for money, Roni was standing inside the room. "I heard all about it from Pam," she said, waving Maddie's explanations away. "Let's get going."

"Boy, thank heavens for your car," Maddie said as they sped off on the country highway to

Western Springs. "This makes things so much easier for me."

"I'm glad," Roni said, glancing over at her friend. "How are you doing?" she asked sympathetically.

"All right. But I'll feel better once I see Aunt Fitty."

"Now where are we going exactly?"

"To Western Springs Community Hospital, I think. The message said the local hospital. If she's not there, we can try St. Joseph's."

"How do I get there?"

"Just drive into Western Springs, and I'll show you from there."

Roni nodded, her auburn curls bouncing. "Will do."

Maddie leaned back against the red leather seat. "I don't want to think about Aunt Fitty right now. Talk to me, Roni."

"What do you want to talk about?"

"Well, for openers, how are you doing?"

"I'm doing . . . better," Roni said thoughtfully.

Maddie sat upright. "You are? Really?"

"Yes, I am. And I guess I have Liz to thank for that."

"Liz? I thought you two didn't get along all that well."

"We didn't, but she helped me through a rough weekend," Roni said.

Maddie immediately felt guilty that she hadn't been around to help Roni through her trauma.

She had been so caught up with school, the play, and her overriding concern about Mike that she wasn't even in touch with her best friends. She felt terrible. She'd been neglecting everyone important to her. "Tell me about it, Roni," she said quietly.

Roin launched into the story of her parents' visit and the tailspin she had gone into that evening. She told Maddie that it had really been Liz's concern that had made her take another look at her actions and decide to seek help.

"So you're going to a counselor now?" Maddie asked.

"Yeah. I've been twice already. It's nice to talk things out with someone who understands. I can see now that the drinking was just a symptom. I've got a lot of feelings to sort out," she said seriously.

"Roni, I know you'll be able to do it," Maddie said confidently.

Roni glanced over at Maddie. "I've got to."

This was such a different side to Roni, serious and direct. Usually Roni was the first person to make a joke or come up with an idea for a prank. "You know," Maddie began, "figuring out the problem is the first real step to solving it, as the saying goes."

"Absolutely," Roni agreed. "I thought I was upset because Zack and I were finished, or because I couldn't room with you guys, but it really all boiled down to how I felt about myself."

"Your parents aren't even the problem. Not really," Maddie said thoughtfully.

"You're right. The counselor and I have discussed that. Once I get my feelings about myself straight, everything else will fall into place. I lost sight of the real Roni Davies for a while, but I'm determined to find her again."

Maddie nodded. "I just hope a little of that nutty personality survives."

Roni flashed her a grin. "Oh, I don't think we have to worry about that. There's definitely a little craziness in the real Roni. I just have to make sure it doesn't crowd out all the rest of me."

The girls' conversation was interrupted by their sudden arrival at the outskirts of Western Springs. Maddie had a vague idea of where the hospital was located, but after dinner they had to stop at a gas station for directions.

After pulling into the hospital parking lot, Maddie hurried through the entance with Roni right behind her. Breathlessly, she asked the front desk for the room number of Fitty Lyons. The sweet-faced secretary at the desk carefully checked her admitting records, but she couldn't find anything that indicated Fitty had been admitted.

"Maybe she's still in the emergency room," Roni suggested.

"That's a possibility," the woman agreed. "Let me just phone over there and check with the nurse on duty."

While the secretary made the call, Maddie tapped her foot impatiently. She wanted to get to Fitty and hold her hand. She remembered all the times her great-aunt had comforted her during childhood injuries and teenage problems. Now Aunt Fitty needed her, and Maddie wanted desperately to be there for her in the same way.

"I'm sorry," the volunteer said, hanging up the phone. "No one with that name has been admitted today."

"I see," Maddie said, but she really didn't. *Where could Fitty be?*

"Have you tried St. Joseph's?"

"No. Can you tell us how to get there?"

The woman gave them explicit instructions, but construction on the highway delayed their trip. Maddie was chewing on her fingernails by the time they arrived at the hospital. "Wait here," Maddie said. "I'll run in and check."

Unfortunately, there were a number of people waiting in line at the information desk, and Maddie suffered through what seemed like an interminable wait. Roni finally came in to see what was holding her up.

When Maddie finally did get to inquire about Fitty, she received the same news that she had at Western Springs Hospital—no one of that name or description had been admitted.

"Now what?" Maddie asked desperately.

"Why don't we just go to your aunt's house? Maybe she was treated and released."

Maddie ran a hand through her hair. "That's a good idea. Let's go."

Fitty lived in a small ranch house set back on a wide expanse of lawn. The house itself was undistinguished, but passers-by couldn't help noticing the beautiful rose bushes that lined the yard. A green thumb was another one of her aunt's attributes.

"It looks deserted," Maddie said unhappily, craning her neck as Roni pulled into the driveway. "The car isn't there, and the door is closed. Aunt Fitty always leaves the door open if she's home."

"Well, let's get out and see. Maybe she's just sleeping or something."

Maddie rapped at the door but no one answered.

Roni peered in the window and shook her head. "I don't think anyone's there."

"Now what?" Maddie said, near tears.

"Let me think for a minute. Are there any neighbors you could ask?"

"I do know the woman down the road. She might know something."

As the girls walked back to the car, Maddie saw a car coming up the road. She blocked the sun with a hand on her forehead and squinted. "I think that's Aunt Fitty's station wagon," she said. "It is!"

Aunt Fitty had hardly gotten out of the car before Maddie smothered her in a big bear hug. "I'm so glad to see you!" she cried.

"Madison," she said, giving her a warm embrace. "What's all this about?"

"How are you feeling, Aunt Fitty?" Maddie looked at her aunt with concern. She certainly didn't appear ill: She was dressed as usual in blue jeans and a faded plaid work shirt. Her blue eyes shone as brightly as ever, and if it wasn't for her silver hair and the tiny crows' feet at the corners of her eyes, she wouldn't look very old at all. "Are you all right?"

"All right? Of course I'm all right. Why shouldn't I be?"

"Maddie got a call saying you'd been taken to the hospital," Roni explained. "She was worried sick herself."

"Why, that's ridiculous," snorted Aunt Fitty. "I haven't been near that hospital—except to visit my friends—in ten years. I make it a policy to stay away from hospitals and doctors. You know that, Maddie," she chided.

"But I don't understand," Maddie said distractedly. "If you weren't sick, why did I get a message saying you were?"

"Well, let's not stay out here and talk about it," Fitty said, herding both girls into the house. "The least I can do is fix you a cup of tea and some cookies after all that running around."

Maddie checked her watch. It was almost five, but even with a short visit, she might be able to make the dance if Mike didn't mind being a little late.

While Aunt Fitty was steeping the tea and

setting out the cookies, Maddie called Mike's dorm and waited for him or his roommate to pick up the phone. After ten rings she disappointedly put down the receiver. She would just have to try him again when she got back to Hawthorne.

"Roni's been telling me about this message you got," Aunt Fitty said as Maddie curled up in an old wooden rocker. "I don't understand this at all. Could it have been a joke, honey?"

Maddie was indignant. "Who would make a horrible joke like that?" She took a sip of the warming chamomile tea. Aunt Fitty always said it was a good, calming drink. But then something awful occurred to Maddie. No one would do this as a joke, but somebody . . . somebody like Erica . . . might just do this on purpose— if she had a good enough reason. And getting Maddie out of the way on the night of Fall Ball would be a very good reason, indeed.

"Aunt Fitty," Maddie said, rising to her feet, "I think we have to go."

"Oh, do you?" Aunt Fitty asked with real disappointment in her voice. "It's been at least a month since we've had a good chance to chat."

Maddie was torn: She had been promising herself she'd come out to visit her great-aunt, and she'd never even called. It was important to get back and try and catch Mike, yes, but Maddie also realized she owed her aunt the courtesy of a longer visit. She sank back into her seat. "I guess I can stay for a little while longer. Tell me what you've got in your garden this fall."

A half hour later, feeling good about her decision to stay, Maddie said good-bye. She tried Mike's dorm once more before she left, but there was still no answer. She'd just have to wait until she got back to talk to him about what had happened.

On the ride home, Maddie shared her suspicions about Erica with Roni. She told her about some of the odd coincidences that seemed to occur whenever Erica was around.

"You think she's behind this wild-goose chase?" Roni asked, shocked.

"It all seems pretty suspicious when you think about it," Maddie said grimly. "A call saying my aunt's sick when she's perfectly fine? Come on, things like that don't just happen. They're planned."

"You're right," Roni agreed slowly. "This was a totally orchestrated event. Now you just have to find out who the conductor was."

Maddie was pretty sure who had written the score this time.

Chapter 14

Maddie looked at the clock again. It was only five minutes later than the last time she had checked, a quarter after twelve.

It has been a long day, she thought to herself, stifling a yawn. She had hurried over to Mike's dorm as soon as she had gotten home from Western Springs, but he wasn't there. From what his resident adviser had said, he had left looking as though he was going to the dance. Erica, too, was gone; and makeup, stockings, and clothes were strewn all over her bedroom. It seemed as though she had suddenly found a date for the evening, too.

Roni had stayed with Maddie most of the evening. They had bought a pizza to eat in front of the TV; but finally, all the driving and the pizza caught up with Roni, and she had started to fall asleep on the couch.

"Go to bed," Maddie urged. "I'll wait up for Erica. Besides, when she finally does come home, we need to be alone."

Roni nodded sleepily. "Wake me up for breakfast," Roni said as she got up, stretched, and headed for the door. "I want to hear how all this comes out."

Jean had drifted in a half hour later and went right to bed. Maddie could hear her removing Erica's junk from her chair, dresser, and bed. Then Stacy had called, saying she was spending the night with Pete's family. Maddie didn't tell her anything about her awful day. She didn't want to ruin Stacy's weekend. It was all she could do to keep her own eyes open, but she was determined to sit right on the couch until Erica walked through the door.

She didn't have to wait too much longer. About twelve-thirty Erica strolled through the front door, disheveled and carrying her pink pumps in her hand. Erica looked shocked to see Maddie sitting there, but she quickly regained her composure. "Maddie, what are you doing up so late?" she asked sweetly. "Studying?"

Maddie's lips tightened. "Where are *you* coming from so late?"

Erica sat down and looked at Maddie with her big brown eyes. "I have a confession to make, Maddie," she said. "I was out with Mike."

"Really? Then your plan must have worked."

"My *plan*?" Erica asked innocently.

"Sure. The-call-Maddie,-worry-her-sick-about-her-aunt,-get-her-out-of-town,-and-have-Mike-take-you-to-the-dance-plan."

Erica got up. "It's late, Maddie and I don't want to listen to wild accusations—"

"Sit down, Erica." When Erica hesitated, Maddie insisted. "Sit."

Erica sank back down on her chair. "All right, I will talk to you, but only because I feel bad about what's developed between me and Mike."

"Yeah, I'm sure you feel just terrible about it."

"I won't lie to you, Maddie. Mike and I, well we . . . feel a powerful attraction for each other."

"So I can see," Maddie said, giving her the once-over.

"But it's something that just happened. We didn't plan it."

"It's something that wouldn't have happened if I hadn't been called out of town," Maddie lashed out.

"You can't blame me for that. I heard your great-aunt was sick. That's not my fault, surely."

"My aunt wasn't sick, and you know it. Of course, it took me visits to two hospitals and a stop at her house to make sure of that. Just enough time for you to go to the dance with Mike."

"I merely went over to Mike's to make sure he knew you had an emergency."

Maddie folded her arms. "So after you did your good deed, then what?"

"Then he asked me who I was going to the dance with, and I told him I didn't have a date. It seemed a shame for both of us to be sitting home, so we decided to go out to dinner. Then we wound up at the dance."

"You look like you went somewhere after the dance, too," Maddie prompted.

"That's none of your business," Erica flared.

"Oh, excuse me," Maddie said, raising her voice. "You steal my boyfriend and it's none of my business?"

"Apparently, he wasn't yours to begin with, or this never would have happened."

"How could you?" Maddie hissed. She stood up and paced the floor nervously. "Do you know how worried I was today when I couldn't find my aunt? How could you possibly be so cruel?"

"I don't know what you're talking about," Erica whispered back angrily.

"Who else would call and tell me my aunt was sick? Who else would *do* something like that?!" she yelled.

"I have no idea who your enemies are, Maddie. Someone was just playing a trick on you. It could have been anybody." Erica countered, just as loudly.

Maddie was usually slow to anger, but she felt as though she were going to explode. "It wasn't *anybody*! It was you!"

Jean suddenly appeared in the doorway.

"What's going on here?" she said, rubbing her eyes. "You're going to wake up the whole dorm."

Maddie threw a poisonous look at Erica. "Frankly, I don't care."

"Well, I do," Jean said.

Using Jean's presence as a diversion, Erica picked up her shoes and headed toward the bedroom. "I'm going to sleep. We can talk about this tomorrow when you're more rational."

Maddie started to stalk after her, but Jean put up a restraining hand. "Maddie, I don't know what's happened here, but believe me, Erica's right. It would be better to talk about this in the morning."

"All right," Maddie said finally, "but you'd better get a good night's sleep, Erica. You're going to need it!" Erica didn't wait for Maddie's reply. She hurried into the bathroom and locked the door behind her. A long, luxurious bath would be a perfect finish for this evening. Sprinkling a handful of expensive bath crystals into the tub, Erica congratulated herself on how beautifully her plan had worked. There had been a few tricky moments, but nothing she couldn't handle.

As she lowered her lithe body into the bubbling water, Erica's thoughts floated back to this morning. It was after Jean had left the suite, and while Maddie was still sleeping soundly, that Erica had carefully lifted the receiver off the phone, just slightly, as though somone hadn't replaced it properly. Then she had hurried over to Kitty's dorm. *It had been a stroke of genius,* Erica thought as she soaked in the tub, *to have Kitty make the call about Aunt Fitty. Chances are slim that Pam would have recognized my voice, but you never can tell.*

Erica had to admit that she had felt a little guilty about pretending some old woman was sick, but she steeled her nerve and told herself it was all for a good cause. Besides, it wasn't as if this Fitty person had really been ill. Maddie found out everything was all right in the end. Except of course that she no longer had a date for the dance with Mike.

Once the call was taken care of, the rest had been simple. About three o'clock she had gone over to Mike's dorm, to make sure he knew about Maddie's predicament. He had been reading his chem textbook under one of the weeping willow trees behind his dorm.

After Erica broke the news, Mike said, "I got a garbled message to that effect. She's going to try to make it back in time for the dance, though."

"I wouldn't count on it," Erica advised. "Roni talked to Pam and said they were having trouble locating the right hospital. And once they do . . . well, who knows what they'll find?" she said dramatically.

"You could be right," Mike said thoughtfully.

Erica clasped her hands around her knees and looked away. "It's a real shame to miss the first dance of the year. For both of you, I mean."

"Who are you going with?" Mike asked.

Erica looked down at her hands shyly. "Oh, I'm not going."

"You're kidding. Why not?"

"Don't make me spell it out, Mike. I don't have a date." She diplomatically neglected to mention that she had turned down three potential suitors.

"The guys on this campus must be nuts," Mike said, shaking his head. "Or else they need glasses."

Erica gave a throaty laugh. "I don't know about that."

"Well, I do." Mike said firmly. "I can't believe you're just going to be sitting home tonight."

"I did sort of want to go," Erica said wistfully.

Erica watched carefully as Mike took the bait. "Say, if Maddie isn't going to make it back in time and you're free, maybe we could run over there together."

"Do you think Maddie would mind?" Erica asked, her eyes wide.

"I don't see why. I mean, I'm sure she'd agree that there's no point in both of us staying home alone."

"Well, if you really think so," Erica said doubtfully.

"Oh, I do," Mike warmed to the idea. "And if Maddie gets home later, she can join us."

Erica hadn't liked the sound of that, but she knew there was no way Mike would have another girl on his mind tonight, not after she was through. "All right." Erica sighed. "But if I'm going out tonight, I'd better go home and get ready."

"How about dinner first," Mike asked. "I borrowed a car from a friend. We can drive over to Jake's."

This was even better than Erica had planned. Now they'd be long gone before Maddie ever got home. "Let's do it," she said, flashing Mike an award-winning smile.

She had flown back to the dorm and dressed as fast as she could for her big evening. She wanted to make sure she was out of the suite before anyone saw her. Out of her closet came the short, pink strapless dress she had brought from New York. Erica thought she looked luscious, and she intended for Mike to feel the same way about her.

That evening, with one sweeping look, he took her in from head to toe. Her hair was pulled back over one ear and held by a pink satin flower. The dress hugged her curvaceous figure, its mini length showing off her shapely legs. She wore her highest pink heels, but they didn't put her anywhere near Mike's height.

"You look unbelievably gorgeous," Mike said, his eyes devouring her. At that very instant, Erica knew Mike was hooked. She'd seen the signs before.

They had a fabulous dinner at Jake's. Erica had mentioned her father's importance in the advertising industry more than once, and then she let slip that he was on the board of the theater group that performed Shakespeare in Central Park. Erica had guessed correctly about Mike: He was a nice guy, true, but he was also a fiercely ambitious one. Mike's interest in Erica became even more evident as she told him how her father liked to help talented people.

After a long and romantic ride around the lake, they had finally gotten around to going to the dance. Erica had almost laughed out loud at the amateurish decorations, but the music was decent and swaying in Mike's arms was heaven. It didn't really matter that she was in a silly gym out in the Georgia boondocks. She was with Mike, and that was enough.

"How about getting out of here?" he had whispered huskily in her ear.

"Where do you want to go?" she asked, pulling back and eyeing him seductively.

"My roommate's gone for the weekend."

"Oh. Is that so?"

He brushed his lips across her throat and ear. "We could be all alone."

"Am I safe with you?"

"I doubt it."

"Mmm . . . well, maybe we could go there for a little while."

Mike had given her one last, lingering kiss, then steered her toward the exit. Erica had had a very clear idea of how far things were going to go, and it wasn't nearly as far as Mike supposed. Still, the hours together had been delightful and stopping Mike before things got too involved would only make him hungry for more.

As she remembered, Erica leaned back in the warm water. She smiled as she thought of Mike's kisses. Maddie might be angry, but it hardly mattered—Mike and Maddie were a thing of the past. Erica scooped up a handful of bubbles and blew them into the air. There was no doubt about it, she had him now.

Chapter 15

Maddie knew that she should get a good night's sleep to get in shape for her confrontation, but her pent-up anger kept her stomach churning and her eyes wide open for most of the night. She finally fell asleep about five, and by the time she woke up, Erica was gone. For the second day in a row, Erica had slipped out while she was sleeping.

Disappointed, she fixed herself a cup of coffee. She had only taken a few sips when the phone rang. Maddie could not have been more surprised to hear Mike's voice at the other end.

"Maddie," he began hesitantly, "I think we need to talk."

"I don't think there's anything left to talk about," Maddie said. She wished she could be harsher or more sarcastic, but Mike's voice still had an effect on her she couldn't deny.

"I'll be over in a few minutes. Please wait there for me." Maddie was left standing there, listening to the steady buzz of the disconnected line in her ear.

From force of habit, she changed into an attractive polka-dot sundress, combed her hair, and put on some makeup. She thought she might as well show Mike what he was missing but inside she was miserable, cursing herself for being stupid enough to lose Mike.

Maddie had just finished applying her makeup when she heard Mike's familiar rap on the door. "Hi, Maddie," he said, not quite looking her in the eye.

"Erica asked me to come over," he said, perching himself on the arm of a chair.

All of Maddie's anger from the previous day came flooding back. "Erica?" she asked, trying to keep her voice under control. "So that's where she went this morning. I wanted to talk to her, and she was with you. That's just perfect."

Mike ran his hand through his hair. "This isn't Erica's fault, Maddie. I realize now I've been attracted to her for a while now, but it wasn't until circumstances threw us together—"

"Circumstances?" Maddie interrupted. "Is that what you think it was? Did Erica bother to tell you she was the one who placed that fake call about my aunt? My aunt wasn't sick at all."

"Erica did tell me you think she was responsible," Mike said carefully, "but she was almost crying when she told me she didn't do it."

"And you believe her."

"Yes, I do."

"I've always heard love is blind," Maddie said bitterly. "I guess it's true. Or maybe love is just stupid."

"Maddie!"

Good, Maddie thought with satisfaction, *I've shocked him.* Sweet little Maddie had opened her mouth for a change. "Sorry, that's how I feel."

"Maddie, I can see that you're hurt, but really, you and I haven't been seeing each other all that long. And I don't mean to criticize, but you've changed since we started dating."

"Changed? I don't know what you mean." But Maddie was afraid she did.

Mike shook his head. "When I first met you, you were sort of sweet and shy. Then, all of a sudden, you were trying so hard to be hip. It wasn't you, and I tried to tell you I liked you the way you were, but you seemed determined to be more sophisticated or something."

Maddie tried not to show it, but a flood of shame washed over her when she heard Mike's words. When she thought of how much time and money she had put into changing her image, and now, just as Stacy had suggested all along, Mike liked her the way she was. Mike *had* liked her, she corrected herself. Maddie was upset, but she wasn't about to show Mike she thought he was right. "I suppose you think Erica is sweet and shy," she said.

"There's a part of her that is, yes."

"Well, that's where you're wrong, Mike. Erica is the most calculating, self-centered person I've ever run across. She'll only hang on to you until something better comes along."

Mike stood up. "Maddie, I'd hoped we could still be friends, but I really don't want to sit here and listen to you bad-mouth Erica. This thing between me and her—it just happened. I wish you hadn't gotten hurt in the process, but all I can say is, I'm sorry."

"Whatever you say. But just remember what I told you. Erica Martin isn't what you think she is. And some day, believe me, you're going to find that out."

After Mike left, Maddie stood there for a moment or two just staring at the door. Then she threw herself down on the couch and cried harder than she had in months.

Stacy found Maddie sniffling an hour later. She coaxed the whole story out of her and sympathized completely, though she couldn't believe Erica was such a witch until after she heard everything. Then she agreed wholeheartedly.

She handed the red-eyed, red-nosed Maddie a tissue and said, "All right, that's it. Pull yourself together while I round up Sam and Roni. We're taking you out to lunch."

"Lunch?" Maddie wailed. "I don't want to eat."

"What do you want to do?" Stacy asked. "Stay curled up on the couch for the rest of your life?"

Maddie nodded mutely.

"Well, you can't. And I think a good way to get you out of your depression is to be with friends."

Stacy wouldn't take no for a answer, so half an hour later Maddie found herself in a corner booth of the Eatery, surrounded by Sam, Roni, and Stacy, all enormously supportive, and all furious with Erica.

"And when I think of all you did for her," Sam said indignantly. "Taking her over to the theater group . . ."

"Don't forget about APA," Stacy said grimly. "She was smart enough to make her move on Mike *after* she got into the sorority."

"If she had just shown her true colors earlier," Roni said, "you could have blackballed her."

Maddie shook her head. "She had this all planned to the last detail. Erica wasn't about to jeopardize her chances of getting into the sorority of her choice. She always gets what she wants—that's the bottom line, right?"

"Mike'll wise up soon enough," Sam predicted.

"Maybe, but he won't want me back." Maddie's eyes filled with tears. "He's already made it perfectly clear that he didn't like me."

"He didn't like who you were *pretending* to be," Stacy corrected.

Maddie used the edge of her napkin to dab away a tear. "Well, I certainly learned one thing from this. I've got to be myself. It's one thing to be rejected for your own personality, but it was my phony sophisticated self that turned Mike off."

"Face it, Maddie, you're sweet and adorable and you're just going to have to live the rest of your life like that," Roni said, patting her hand.

Maddie smiled through her tears. "I just feel like such an idiot."

"Well, you shouldn't," Sam declared. "It sounds to me like you were hustled by one of the best."

"And I for one don't intend to let her get away with it," Stacy said, pounding the table with her fist.

Maddie sat up straight. "No, don't start anything."

"What do you mean?"

"I remember what we went through last semester when we were all fighting. I don't want to start living in an armed camp again."

"Don't tell me you're just going to pretend nothing happened!" Stacy said, shocked.

"If you mean am I going to be friendly, the answer is no," Maddie told her. "I'm going to try to ignore her. I hope we're not around the stuite at the same time very often. But I don't want to start a war over this, Stacy."

"Maddie, I think you're carrying niceness a little too far," Sam protested.

"I don't," Roni said unexpectedly. "The big

lesson I've learned in the last couple of weeks is that you've got to be true to yourself. Being nasty is hard for Maddie: She doesn't want to act that way. It's not natural, and it would make her even more unhappy."

"You do understand." Grateful, Maddie smiled.

"And you would hate yourself more than you dislike Erica," Sam said, slowly comprehending.

"That's right. I'd be walking around trying to think of sarcastic things to say, Erica wouldn't even care, and I'd just feel like a mean person."

"I don't know," a doubtful Stacy said. "I still think Erica is getting away awfully easily."

"Maybe," Maddie said, now more serene, "but remember, she still has to live with herself."

"That won't bother her," Stacy grumbled.

"Not today, or next week, but you can't be mean and calculating like that forever and not have it catch up with you."

The girls were silent for a moment or two. Then Sam spoke up. "Well, Stacy, it sounds to me like while you and I were just going to class, Roni and Maddie here were getting an intensive education in self-knowledge."

Stacy nodded. "Yes. And I'd have to give them an A."

Maddie smiled around the table at her friends. This hadn't been the easiest month of her life, and she wouldn't want to repeat it for anything. But Sam was right: She had learned some valuable lessons, and they weren't the kinds of things taught in class. "Just give me an honorary diploma from the College of Hard Knocks," she said with a wry laugh. "But I'll tell you one thing. I have no intention of going to graduate school!"

"I think Erica Martin will be taking a class or two at that college," Roni promised. "After all, her freshman year has only just begun."

Here's a sneak preview of *Class Act*, book number ten in the continuing ROOMMATES series from Ivy Books.

All of a sudden Angie heard thundering footsteps and wondered who was making so much noise in the library. When Aaron Goldberg stormed around the corner with an angry look on his face, Angie couldn't believe he was actually heading in her direction.

Aaron held the Hawthorne newspaper in front of her face. "How could you do this?" he demanded.

"Excuse me?" Angie didn't have the slightest idea what had made him so upset. "What's the problem?"

"You said you couldn't help with the rally because the whole thing upset your *vibes!*"

"Shhh. . . ." He was hushed by people from all directions.

"This isn't the place," Angie suggested meekly.

"Well, I'll leave if you can explain to me how your *vibes*—"

"Aaron Goldberg!" the librarian barked, almost running to get to the source of the disturbance. "You know better than this! How can anyone work in here with you making so much noise?"

Aaron grabbed Angie's wrist and she barely
had time to collect her things before he dragged
her outside. He didn't even bother to look for a
private spot. He just started yelling at her in the
middle of the sidewalk.

"Explain to me why you couldn't work on a
rally meant to make the campus a safer place for
everyone, but you can try to put together some
scatterbrained plan to collect garbage along the
nature trail to make it a *neater* place for
everyone!"

"Aaron," she said from between clenched
teeth. "You're attracting a crowd."

"I don't care if Dan Rather covers it for the
evening news, I want you to explain to me how a
bunch of trees and bushes are more important
than people!"

Angie squinted at the people circling her and
Aaron. Did this constitute publicity for her
clean-up project? She'd have to ask Professor
Stevens, because she wasn't quite sure.

"What's wrong, Angie Perelli? I bet you're so
quiet because you can't defend your actions."

She tipped her head back and stared right into
his dark eyes. "I don't think there's anything
wrong with my trail project. If we each don't do
our part to take care of our world, do you know
what's going to happen? We're not going to have
any world left to live in!"

"So you'd say clean hiking trails are more
important than human dignity?"

"Of course not."

"But you *are* saying that," Aaron said with a sly smile. "You're telling me that if we don't clean up that trail Saturday morning, it's going to destroy the earth. I can only conclude that it's foolish for me to worry about improving human conditions if it's all over for us anyway."

"You're making fun of me," Angie complained. Aaron was twisting her words. They were both doing important things, and there was no reason they should be competing with each other.

"I'm not laughing at you, Angie," he deadpanned. "Not now that you've explained it all to me. Where do I sign up? I want to help you save the world."

"Aaron Goldberg!" She was too mad for a minute to get her thoughts straight. "Just when I started thinking you were the nice, concerned citizen everyone says you are, you have proved once again what a jerk you are!" Angie practically yelled.

"Are you saying you won't let me help?" Aaron asked, feigning disappointment. "But my *vibes* tell me I should go out and buy some trash bags right now."

"You can't help. You're not a freshman," she grumbled.

"Now you're throwing bureaucracy in my face!" His mouth fell open in disbelief. "I'm so disappointed in you. After Saturday night—"

Aaron was interrupted by catcalls from the crowd that had gathered; they wanted to know what had happened between the pair Saturday night. Angie had visions of trying to explain not just this scene, but last Saturday night, to her roommate Sam.

Aaron ignored the hecklers. "After our talk, I was starting to think you were a real person. But you're coming from another world, or maybe another planet. You don't make any sense. Think about it."

He stalked off, leaving Angie alone in the midst of some very curious spectators. She knew there was no way to salvage her cause or her reputation at that moment. These people had known Aaron for a long time and she was the new kid on the block. The best she could manage was a nervous laugh as she walked off in the direction of the science building.

"I hear you've had a busy day," Professor Stevens said as soon as Angie stepped into his office.

"You saw the article in the paper," she ventured.

"And I had a first-hand view of your confrontation with Aaron Goldberg." He pointed to the window behind his desk. It overlooked the sidewalk by the library. Angie shifted uncomfortably from foot to foot, and he laughed.

"I wouldn't call it a confrontation, exactly," she said.

"What would you call it?" He took her books out of her hands and placed them on his desk.

"A difference of opinion," she declared, wondering why he'd been so chivalrous.

Professor Stevens laughed again and reached out to close his office door. "Aaron's a pretty popular guy," he said, looking at Angie carefully. "Do you date him?"

"Date him?" she hooted. "The man thinks I'm a refugee from Jupiter. He'd rather date a toad, and I'd rather stay home and read *Moby Dick*."

He nodded. "Then the news of today's little scene should die down quickly. Stories only keep circulating if they involve romance," he guaranteed.

"Good. So what do you think we could be doing to get some positive publicity for the project? Now that I've lost a public debate."

"I'm not sure," he admitted.

"Have you talked to the other science teachers? You said you'd ask them to mention the campaign to their freshman classes," Angie reminded him.

"Oh yeah." He jumped off the desk and came over to stand next to Angie. "I was going to ask them at a department meeting but it was cancelled."

"That's too bad," she said. Professor Stevens seemed a little distracted at times, and Angie wasn't surprised he'd forgotten his promise.

He leaned close to her and took a deep breath. "Your hair smells good. What kind of shampoo do you use?"

"Some natural stuff," she said, disconcerted by his question. She pushed herself off the windowsill and pretended to examine the clippings tacked to his bulletin board. "A friend of mine suggested I make some kind of personal contact with the freshman class. Do you think I should try to get permission to visit some classes?"

He ran a hand through his hair. "That kind of permission is very hard to get." He stared at Angie and muttered something that sounded like, "Unless you have good legs."

Angie told herself she had to be imagining things. "Uh, Professor Stevens—"

"You know something, Angie? You looked really good at the rally last Friday. You should wear yellow more often."

"Look, uh, I've got to get to class now," Angie lied. She had to get out of there; Professor Stevens was acting too weird.

"Don't let me keep you then." He walked her to the door and handed her her books. "I'll see you later." He grinned at her.

Angie hurried down the hall without peeking over her shoulder to see if he was watching her. For some reason, his behavior had really bothered her. But she had to be honest with herself. She was mostly upset because she knew the trail cleanup campaign was going to be a failure. On Saturday morning, she would be the only one on the path, unless a few students decided to take a morning hike, tossing their doughnut wrappers aside as they walked along.